By JU

Suddenly Dating
Suddenly Engaged
Suddenly Single

Lear Family Saga Series
Material Girl
Beauty Queen
Miss Fortune

Highlander Lockhart Series
Highlander Unbound
Highlander in Disguise
Highlander in Love

Over the Edge Series
All I Need is You
One More Night
Fall Into Me

Desperate Debutantes Series
The Hazards of Hunting a Duke
The Perils of Pursuing a Prince
The Dangers of Deceiving a Viscount

The Cabot Sisters Series
The Trouble With Honor
The Devil Takes a Bride
The Scoundrel and the Debutante

Homecoming Ranch Series
Homecoming Ranch
Return to Homecoming Ranch
The Perfect Homecoming

Highland Groom Series
Wild Wicked Scot
Sinful Scottish Laird
Hard-Hearted Highlander

Novellas
A Christmas Secret
The Bridesmaid
One Mad Night

Also Available

In the
Lake Haven Series

Suddenly in Love
Suddenly Dating
Suddenly Engaged
Suddenly Single

SUDDENLY SINGLE

Lake Haven Series, #4

JULIA LONDON

To my friends who help make things happen.
Looking at you, Linda and Teri

One

Weddings were not Edan's thing. Especially not since his own wedding had gone belly-up a couple of months back. Especially not when his attendance required him to wear a tie, like the one actively strangling him. Maybe he'd tightened it when he meant to loosen it. Anything was possible—he'd taken healthy advantage at the reception's open bar in order to forget how much he hated weddings. He'd had a couple of drinks, or ten, who was counting, but enough that a friend had dropped him home, swerving around a Smart car that was parked in front of the old family inn Edan owned and managed.

And was going to sell, just as soon as he could.

In his office, he pulled off his suit coat, then used both hands to try and manhandle the bloody stubborn bit of silk from his neck, managing to tear the tag from the underside of the tie in the process. He was panting with the exertion when he thought he heard something. The walls of the old Victorian residence that was the Cassian Inn were pretty thick, and he couldn't be sure what he'd heard.

There it was again—someone was ringing the little bell at the reception desk.

He flipped through the mental catalog in his sodden brain for who would be ringing the bell. No one. No one should be ringing the bell because there was an enormous sign out front proclaiming the Cassian Inn was closed for new business. Edan was tired, he was grumpy, and he was in no mood to be courteous and cheerful to whoever had ignored his sign.

The perpetrator tapped the bell again. What bloody numpty ignored the closed signs and walked into the reception area anyway? Better yet, what numpty had left the door unlocked? All right, bloody hell, that numpty would be him. Everyone around here knew he often forgot to lock the front door.

Edan scrubbed his face with his fingers.

The bell sounded again, *ding ding.*

Whoever it was ought to at least allow a minute or two to see if the first dings would be answered before tapping again. But no, Whoever did not wait, and just for that, Whoever could do the waiting. Edan unbuckled his sporran and tossed it onto his chair. Rosalyn, the bride, had begged him to wear a formal kilt, because God forbid a Scotsman show up at any American event in anything other than a kilt. "The girls *love* it," Rosalyn had gushed.

The girls did love it.

Whoever now saw fit to pound the daylight from

the little silver reception bell. Or at least it seemed that way to Edan's throbbing head. All right then, he didn't particularly want a contretemps, but he'd bloody well have a go all the same. He marched out of the offices and strode down the hall to the reception area.

But he hesitated with his first step through the door. He didn't know who exactly he'd expected—an impatient elderly couple, as was wont to wander these parts—but he had not expected the lovely young woman in the hiking boots, the alarmingly short shorts, and her caramel-colored tangle of hair tied up rather haphazardly in a silk scarf.

"Oh! Hello!" she said with great exuberance and surprise when she spotted him. Her finger, Edan noticed, was poised precariously above the silver bell's little knocker. "I didn't think anyone was here!"

"Perhaps because the sign at the door states we are closed?" he asked curtly.

She blinked. Her finger slowly receded from the ringer. "Irish?"

"Pardon?"

"Your accent. Irish?"

If this pretty interloper thought she could simply employ a master level deflection technique on him, she was wrong. "No' Irish. May I help you? We're closed."

"Scottish!" she said triumphantly. "Of *course*, you're wearing a kilt! I didn't notice it at first." She smiled. "Nice kilt, by the way."

What in bloody hell was this woman doing out here on a Sunday evening trying to guess his ethnicity? No one came this far around the lake on Sundays, unless it was an ambulance on its way to the care home up the road. She had a rather large bag strapped to her back, and attached to that was a rolled-up yoga mat. Jesus, she wasn't one of those hippies who occasionally appeared at the lake around the time of the music festival, was she? Last year, some of the tools from the shed had gone missing after a tribe of hippies had sauntered through, leaving a trail of marijuana smoke behind them. That was the problem with this inn. Lake Haven was the playground of the rich and famous, who could reach it by train from New York City in an hour. But no one came around to the less popular side of the lake except old people and shifty-types and people who wanted to relive Woodstock. Was she a celebrity, then? From time to time celebrities seeking to escape appeared with enormous dark glasses and knit caps and cigarettes dangling from their lips.

"Umm...so anyway, you're wearing a kilt, and you have a very nice but very not-American accent, so I'm going to have to assume I'm right and hope that you have a room available?"

Edan opened his mouth to answer, but that question made absolutely no sense.

"Actually," she said, holding up a slender finger, "I don't just hope it. I'm praying for it. Like...*really* praying. It's been an insanely long day."

Edan was about to remind her the establishment was closed—PER THE SIGN—but she rubbed her earlobe in a manner that suggested she was a wee bit nervous. For some ridiculous reason, that gave him pause. She seemed a tiny bit fearful. It shouldn't matter to him—he was closed. He was closed, he was closing for good, he was so closed he'd locked up most of the bedding. That being said, it wasn't impossible to give her a room. It was quite possible, actually. He still had his final two bookings arriving this week. All he had to do was hand her a key. But it was the principle of the thing! One did not appear at a closed inn and demand entrance. One did *not.*

But before he could think it all the way through, she said, quite needlessly, "I know I don't have a reservation. Unfortunately, I've been forced against my will to pass through town." She paused, as if rethinking that. "Well," she said with a slight shrug, "not exactly pass through. I hadn't planned to come *here* at all. Not that I wouldn't come here, because this inn is *darling,* but the truth is that circumstances have sort of put me in, what do you call it," she said, making a whirring motion with her hand. "Dire straits." One fine brow rose hopefully above the other.

Edan flicked his gaze over her. He noted her excellent figure because he was a man and it was impossible not to notice a figure like that, especially after several whiskies. Long, slender legs. A waist that curved perfectly into hips. Breasts that were neither too big nor too small. She was physical appealing. But that did no make him suddenly interested in her unfortunate event, because he was developing a massive hangover as he stood, his inn days were all but over, and he still hadn't gotten past his annoyance that she'd ignored the sign he'd labored over.

On the other hand, it was rather late, and the last thing he wanted to do was argue, or be the one to put out a woman all alone into the night. Frankly, he'd sooner have this over and done than prolong the agony of standing here. So he reached for the ledger.

"Not that this isn't a beautiful place," she said, holding up a hand. "I don't mean that *this* is the dire straits."

What? Did anything she say make sense?

"It's *gorgeous*," she added, a little too enthusiastically. "But I had this change of plans at the last minute, and I got a ride from a friend—well, not a friend, exactly, but a friend of a friend...I think. Actually, I'm not sure who he was. Anyway, he was on his way home, and apparently he lives up in the hills somewhere, at a compound from the sound of it if I'm being honest, and he wasn't going all the way to East Beach, but he mentioned an inn where I could definitely get a room, because he said no one ever stayed here, but that maybe I should call someone in East Beach first, because if he let me off here, no Uber was going to pick me up, and all the cabs are in Black Springs, and you're, like, *really* off the beaten path, you know?"

Jesus, this woman could natter on. He stared at her impatiently. Her cheeks pinkened and she said quickly, "*Anyway.* I really hope you have a room, because if you don't, I'll have to sleep on one of the benches outside." She smiled in that way women had of smiling when they thought something was too preposterous to even contemplate.

It was not too preposterous to contemplate.

But Edan glanced down at the ledger and thought of the rooms. He'd been systematically going through them, stripping the beds, storing the linens, turning off the toilets. He was about halfway through the mansion, but there were some rooms around back he'd not yet cleared, leaving them open for the final bookings. "How long?"

"On the bench?"

He looked up. "Just the night, then?"

"That's a start," she said, and laughed nervously as she pointed a red-tipped finger at him and said, "*That,* sir, is an interesting question. You know what's funny?"

"No' as yet."

"What's funny is, I might need more than one night. I mean, if you don't mind. Well, you probably do, but the thing is, I don't exactly know how long."

How could she not know? He tilted his head to one side and studied her a little more closely. "Are you homeless?"

"*Homeless!*" She laughed, too loudly and too long, and then sobered a little. "Sort of," she admitted. "I mean, not *technically.* But sort of."

She didn't really look homeless. She looked like the type of woman who appeared in advertisements for feminine hygiene products, all pretty and fresh.

"Wait—I am *not* homeless, if that's what you think. I *have* a home," she said adamantly, pressing her hand to her chest in earnestness. "But it's in California. I've been on a road trip with a guy I thought was...well, I thought he was something he is not, and he surprised me, but not in a good way, and now, I'm suddenly single!" she exclaimed, casting both arms wide, as if announcing she was actually a celebrity he ought to know.

Edan didn't know what he was supposed to say to what sounded like a right bloody mess. "Why do you no' go home, then?" he asked curiously.

"It's complicated."

She was a hippie, all right, and it didn't sound like she was planning a short stay. He would give her one night. Two at most. One night to nurse her wounds, one to figure out how to get to East Beach, the trendy tourist village on the other side of the lake, or wherever she intended to go next. The Woodstock shrine, probably. All things considered, giving her a room was really very decent of him. After he booked her in, he'd give himself a healthy pat on the back.

She tugged nervously at a thick strand of wavy hair. "I mean, there is obviously more to the story, but I didn't figure you'd want the play-by-play."

She figured correctly.

She pressed her lips together. "But you're really open, right?"

Lord. "No. Just as the rather large sign on the entrance indicates, aye?"

She tried to look surprised. "What sign?"

He pointed.

"I didn't see a sign," she said without looking in the direction he pointed.

He arched a brow.

"Okay, I saw the sign," she admitted, deflating a little. "I was hoping I could talk my way in. I'm just really stuck, Mr... ?"

"Mackenzie."

"I'm really stuck, Mr. Mackenzie. My mind is spinning and I really don't know what to do with myself. This breakup was very inopportune, you know?"

He didn't really, because he'd never heard anyone describe a breakup as *inopportune.* Was there such a thing as an opportun*e* breakup? But then again, maybe he did understand, because come to think of it, his breakup had been spectacularly inopportune. The wedding venue had been booked. Tickets had been purchased. Gowns had been bought.

She didn't wait for him to muddle through to his

answer. She suddenly melted onto his countertop, spreading her arms across the surface and resting one cheek against it. "This is a *disaster*," she moaned.

"It's quite—"

"You're right, I'm being totally unreasonable."

He hadn't said that.

"I'll just park on your bench for the night. I don't suppose you have a blanket I could borrow? Or maybe a pillow or something? If you don't have a pillow, that's okay. I'll just use my bag. It's soft," she said. "Except for the bottom, maybe, where I have my laptop and cords. But I can—"

"Miss, I'll give you a room," he said.

She gasped. She lifted her head. "You *will*? Ohmigod, thank you *so much*."

"But for the night, aye? No more than two."

"Right, a week at the very most. I really appreciate it." She carelessly let her bag and yoga mat fall off her shoulder to the floor with a sudden laugh. "There for a minute, I thought it was me and that bench."

He took a registration card from the box. "I'll need a bank card."

"Sure. I happen to have one right here." She leaned down and rummaged around in her bag, then stood up with her wallet and opened it. The little embroidered pink thing held more cards than a bloody bank. She eyed a few, settled on one, and handed it to him.

He handed her the registration card and a pen, took her bank card and ran it through the machine.

"You're a lifesaver, Mr. Mackenzie," she said as she filled out the card. "You know, I loved this place the moment I saw it."

"It was dark when you first saw it," he reminded her. He looked at the bank card: *Jennifer Turner.* He began to enter information into the ancient computer system he would be happy to abandon when he returned to Scotland. He handed her the card. She did have nice legs. He'd always been attracted to nice legs. And eyes. Aye, he appreciated lovely blue eyes like hers. And breasts—well, obviously, he liked those a lot. And bums. And hair, and—

"I can't believe more people don't live on this side of the lake," she said. The woman was clearly much at ease chatting with only herself. "I'd buy a house here if I could. I'd have a little cottage with window boxes full of flowers by the lake. Cottages always look so tranquil, but you don't see them much anymore. Everything has to be ginormous, have you noticed that? What's wrong with small and cozy, I ask you?"

Good God. Surely she'd take a breath before long. He turned around to a board and lifted a key from one of the pegs.

"But you know how it is, you find a place and you really dig it. I have to say, I'm getting a great vibe from this inn. You must have, too, at some point, right? I mean, is that why you're here?"

He handed her the key. "Room 215. Turn right at the end of the hall." He pointed.

"Great! Thank you." Jennifer Turner picked up her bags. She started in the direction he'd indicated, then paused and glanced back at him. "Is it too late to place an order with room service?"

"*Room* service?" he echoed incredulously. She could not possibly think he'd open the dining room for her, too.

Jennifer winced. "Do you think I could get something to eat? Maybe a sandwich? I'm *starving*. I've only had a bag of chips today."

"The dining room is closed," he said impassively as he glanced at his watch. Actually, a sandwich sounded quite good. Perhaps he'd make one for himself once she stopped talking, if that was even possible, and went on to her room.

"Ah. Okay." She pressed a hand to her abdomen. "I'll just…eat my shoe or something. I don't know why I didn't think to pick up an energy bar in case of an emergency. My friend Brooke always has one in her purse. She's a *runner*," she said, making quote marks in the air and rolling her eyes. "Which means she won't go near a good burger. I don't know what the point of running is if you can't eat what you want. Give me yoga any day."

Her stomach suddenly let out a wail of hunger. She blushed. "Sorry about that."

Damn it all to bloody hell. Edan sighed. "Aye, then. I'll make you a sandwich."

She made a soft cry of delight. "*Would* you? And maybe some chips?"

Who was this creature who had appeared out of the night to torment him? "Anything else?"

She shrugged. She fidgeted with the strap of her yoga mat. "If you had a cake or a cookie, that would be great. Sugar is my go-to for stress eating."

Well. Edan grudgingly had to respect a fellow stress-eater. "Kitchen is just through those doors," he said, pointing in the opposite direction of her room. "Come at half past the hour."

"Thank you!" She picked up her bag and yoga mat and started in the direction of her room. "We're not dressing for dinner, are we?" She laughed at his expression and said, "Kidding!" and then disappeared.

Right. Well this was going to be an interesting pair of days from the look of things.

But a ham sandwich and crisps sounded like the perfect thing to soak up the whisky hangover that had melted over Edan's brain. And frankly, he, too, wondered if there was any cake.

Two

———◆———

Jenny closed the door of room 215 softly behind her, dropped her bag and her yoga mat…and then fell face down onto the bed, her arms splayed from end to end.

What. The. Hell?

Had she *really* just yapped her way into a room at a closed inn? She didn't know whether to be appalled or proud. Of *course* she'd seen the sign that said the inn was closed. No one could miss that damn sign— all it lacked was a skull and crossbones. But the thought of spending the night on that bench or the side of the road had made her desperate. Or walking the five miles around the lake to East Beach.

This might possibly be the dumbest thing she had ever done. Not talking her way into the room—that had been genius, thank you. But taking off with Devin on this summer "trip."

"You are one lucky idiot," she muttered into the bedspread.

She pushed up to her elbows, swept her hair from her eyes and thought about the man behind the reception desk who looked like he'd just walked off the set of *Outlander*. How was it that someone that hot, wearing a kilt no less, could be tucked away in this old inn on the wrong side of the lake? He was awfully tight-lipped. But she could forgive his curtness because those lips made her blood rush hot and his eyes were so green and piercing.

He was the perfect person to meet after throwing her canteen at Devin.

Devin, Jesus. She was emotionally exhausted and furious with herself about that.

Jenny sat up, crossed her legs beneath her, and looked around. The room was tiny, and it smelled like fresh paint. She could see an oversize bathtub in the tiny bathroom—score—and it looked as if the pair of corner windows looked out over...

She shifted forward, straining to see out of the window.

Okay, well, the view was of a storage shed. But beyond the storage shed were the hills around Lake Haven. The setting was pretty, and the inn was charming in a gothic novel kind of way. Especially since it was tended by a mysterious man who rarely spoke, but when he did, it was with a deep and lilting Scottish brogue.

Why was it never she dated guys like Outlander? Why did she always hook up with the feckless Devins of the world?

Feckless. There were far more descriptive words to describe him. Not only had he proven himself entirely worthless—he couldn't even pitch a tent—but he'd also proven himself to be a cheater. With Misty Pachenko, no less. The woman with the buzzed head and oversized denim shirts and excellent tent-pitching skills. Jenny supposed she ought to be grateful that *someone* had known how to do it.

Devin's cheating aside, what really annoyed Jenny about the whole situation was herself. She certainly had not loved Devin, and let's be honest, she couldn't say how much she'd actually liked him after a few solid days in his company. Especially given that his performance between the sheets was vanilla at best. She was glad to be free of him.

But instead of thinking about all the reasons she had ended up with a guy like him and questioning what, exactly, she was doing with her life right now, she was thinking about the cute Outlander. She ought to be at least questioning why she'd *needed* to be in that horrible relationship with Devin, or why she always seemed to need to be in the sort of superficial relationships that were easy to escape. She clearly and desperately needed to examine her head, but she was tired and hungry, and she wanted to get on with the business of eating her feelings, because *come on, Jen, that's what you do so well.*

With a moan, she fell onto her back to stare at the ceiling with a surprising and pretty plaster medallion.

Twelve minutes to sandwich.

Oh, but she could imagine what her friends would say if they were here right now. They'd be full of the *told-you-sos* and *he's-such-a-dicks.* Vanessa and Brooke had warned her, had voiced their unfavorable opinions about her plans to hobo around with Devin this summer. "So irresponsible," said Vanessa, who was supremely responsible.

"How is it that neither of you need a job right now?" asked Brooke, who often proudly reminded them that she'd been working since she was thirteen.

Jenny didn't *need* a job—she had access to plenty of money. She wanted the right one. This camp-across-America trip with Devin and some of his musician friends had seemed like a very good way to think through her options. Just backpacks and tents, Devin had said. Camping in one place and then the next, like a pack of wanderers, playing gigs where they could get them. It had sounded kind of fun.

"It sounds insane," Brooke had said. "I don't get why you're so keen to go. He never comes to see you, Jen. Half the time you can't get him on the phone, he won't answer your texts. And then you sent him five hundred dollars?"

Brooke had shrieked that part.

"It was a loan!" Jenny had shrieked back. Except that she'd known even as the words were flying out of her mouth that she would never get the money back. Well hang her from the highest tree, then—when someone told her they needed help, she helped. Devin was a free spirit, a musician without a muse, a man searching for his place in this world. In some ways, he'd reminded her of her—a liberal arts graduate who knew a whole lot about nothing that mattered, and nothing practical, who had devoted her entire life to taking care of her widowed dad who was a hoarder, and suffered from Parkinson's disease, and needed her. She was all her father had. Well. Until recently.

Ten minutes to sandwich.

The thing was, Jenny could never be as certain about anything as her friends were certain about everything. Maybe that's why she'd always felt like the perpetual spare tire in their merry little band. A barnacle stuck on the boat of their friendship.

She'd gone with Devin because she'd desperately wanted out of Santa Monica. Away from her dad and his overstuffed house and his new girlfriend with the sixteen year-old son. And Jenny could afford to flit aimlessly around the East Coast with a loser like Devin if she wanted to because her father was insanely wealthy and even more insanely generous.

Not that she intended to live off her dad. Nope. She just didn't know what yet. What she'd needed for a very long time was a place to belong. That idea had grown like a weedy vine in her over the last year, covering all her other thoughts and ambitions to do with working and settling down. She needed to be and work where she belonged. She needed some space away from Dad and friends and bad boyfriends to think about being suddenly single and having no firm plan for her life.

So now that the summer of Devin was officially a bust, Jenny had to figure these things out. She didn't want to go back to California, to no job and a family home stuffed to the rafters with junk and new people. She didn't want to teach anymore. She needed something creative. Something big, something complex, something she could sink her teeth into.

Whatever it was, she needed to work it out on her own.

But she couldn't work it out on her own with her stomach growling like it was.

Six minutes to sandwich. An image of Outlander in his kilt making a sandwich flit through her mind's eye.

Yeah, okay, six minutes was close enough. Jenny pushed herself off the bed and picked up her bag and rummaged around inside until she found some palazzo pants and a clean T-shirt, and took those into a bathroom so small she could lift her arms and touch both walls with her elbows.

But there was enough room to freshen up.

She took a look at herself in the mirror. She looked fine. She didn't look lost or desperate or confused. See? This wasn't such a bad idea after all.

Three

———◆———

Jenny made her way down the hall, through the small reception area with the Oriental rug and the rack of brochures, and on through the doors Outlander had indicated earlier. That led to a large dining room. At the other end of the room, light spilled out of an open doorway, and she could hear the sound of a knife against a cutting board.

She moved across the room and peeked inside. It was a kitchen, and there was Outlander, still dressed in a kilt. He'd ditched the vest and had rolled up the sleeves of his dress shirt. He'd donned an apron that said *Good Eats Served Here* and was busily slicing tomatoes on the kitchen island, where a variety of pots and pans hung over his head.

Jenny grabbed onto the doorframe and sort of swung into the room. "*Hey*," she said, trying to sound breezy.

Outlander glanced up, his green-eyed gaze flicking over her. He pointed to a stool at the kitchen island.

She was going to take a wild guess that she was supposed to sit. She walked across the kitchen and slid on to her assigned stool and glanced around her—the kitchen was gleaming white, with black and white tile on the floor that matched the backsplash between the cabinets and kitchen counters. There was an industrial stove with more burners than Jenny could ever imagine uses for, and an enormous refrigerator with glass doors. "Nice kitchen," she said.

He sliced into a block of cheese.

"You must like to cook."

He looked at her strangely. "No' really."

But he was wearing an apron. People who possessed aprons generally liked to cook. She watched him get a loaf of bread from a bread drawer and lay it on a cutting board. The silence between them seemed to grow thicker.

"I really have to thank you again," Jenny said, and absently twirled a thick strand of hair around her finger. "I know it's a huge imposition, but you wouldn't believe the day I've had."

Outlander didn't take the bait. He made a sound like a grunt and sawed into the bread.

"My name is Jenny, by the way," she said.

"Aye, I checked you in."

"Right," she said, and giggled, not because it was funny, but because this couldn't be more awkward. She did not do well with awkward. She had a tendency to take awkward situations and put them on blast with her words. "What's your name? I mean, besides Mr.

Mackenzie."

He hesitated, as if debating whether he should tell her. "Edan," he said quietly.

"That sounds totally Scottish. What do people call you? Ed?"

He paused, as if thinking about it. "I suppose most call me Mr. Mackenzie." He resumed slicing the bread.

"*They call me Mr. Tibbs*," Jenny responded in her best Sidney Portier voice.

Edan stopped sawing to look at her.

"It's from a movie. An old movie. Too old, I guess."

He glanced down.

Jenny flushed. So stuffy! "People call me Jenny. Except my friends. Guess what they call me?"

Edan Mackenzie did not stop slicing bread.

"They call me Turner Tots, or the Jennerator. They used to call me The Jenlanthropist, because I went through this period where I was giving away my worldly goods, which, I will confess, did not last long." It had been one of those times she'd gotten a little frantic she was going to turn out to be a hoarder like her dad and started giving away everything in her cluttered apartment. Brooke had stopped her from giving away her laptop.

Edan Mackenzie gave her a look as if he couldn't figure her out.

Jenny was generally pretty confident in her own skin, but there was something about his steady gaze that made her anxious. She twirled around on the stool to check out the awesome refrigerator. "How long have you worked for the Cassian Inn?" she asked, turning around again when she figured it was safe.

"I own it."

"Own…the hotel?"

"Aye, the hotel. The grounds. The cottages." He shrugged.

So "They-Call-Me-Mr. Mackenzie" owned this old mansion. Wouldn't he make a great movie? Darkly brooding, handsome, and living in a mysterious mansion. A body in room 215…

He looked at her again, and Jenny got a squirmy, not-used-to-people vibe from him. Which was a little strange, because she'd guess that women would be lining up at his door.

Maybe the reason they weren't was the lack of public transportation to his quaint establishment. It seemed a bit too far out of the way. But put this guy in Chicago or Santa Monica or New York, and sheesh, women would pitch their tents and camp out overnight, hold each others' place in line so someone could dash off to Starbucks for a round of Frappuccinos—all to get a run at him.

"Do you live here by yourself?" *First objective: establish his single/not-single status.*

"You're verra curious," he said.

It was called making conversation, but okay, he didn't want to talk about it. "I like your kilt," she said. "I wish American men would wear them. They look really good and they seem practical to me."

He began putting the sandwich together.

"I knew a girl once who fell in love while she was on vacation in Scotland," Jenny said. "He told her kilts are for weddings and funerals."

Edan Mackenzie arranged leaves of lettuce on the bread. He admired his handiwork.

He was going to make her work for every word.

"Sooo...?" she asked, gesturing to his kilt. "Which was it for you?"

"Wedding."

"I love weddings!"

He slapped some ham on top the lettuce, and then a slice of tomato. "Never knew a lass who didna love them."

"That's a gross generalization, sir. I've been a bridesmaid a few times and trust me, I didn't love *that*. I had to wear a hideously pink dress once. The bride said it was champagne, but that thing was so sickly pink the only thing missing was the diabetes warning label. But yeah, okay, I will concede that most of us love weddings. I wouldn't say I'm such a fan of marriage, however." No sooner were the words out of her mouth that she lifted her hand. "Wait. That didn't come out right. I'm not *against* marriage. I just don't think you have to have a piece of paper to be committed." Jesus, more words were leaping off her tongue before Jenny's central control system could put her mouth on lockdown.

Outlander opened a bag of chips and shook a few out onto a plate. He clearly was not going to discuss his views on marriage with a total stranger because *his* central control system was working just fine and had sent everyone home and closed up shop for the night.

Jenny felt a terrible and wholly unnecessary need to clarify. She often felt this need. "I *am* for marriage. I just don't think everyone has to do it. But weddings! Weddings are the best. It's the one time entire families can come together and get dressed up, and be happy and just dance. What's not to love? The last wedding I went to was one of my best friend's. Bethany and Matt."

Outlander was slicing the sandwich in half.

"I was a bridesmaid. But *that* was a beautiful dress." Bethany would kill her if she ever said anything less about that teal-blue halter dress. Jenny hadn't loved it. She suddenly laughed, recalling how she and Vanessa and Brooke had all had too much to drink. They sat at a table envying how happy and beautiful Bethany had looked and complaining about their dresses. Somehow, they'd gotten on the topic of relationships. "At that wedding, my friends and I had this ridiculous conversation about marriage and relationships. We decided we needed to have a list of non-negotiables. Do guys do that?"

"I donna know what you mean," Outlander said.

"You know, your list of must-haves in a partner."

He shook his head.

"Like, you're saying that the person you date has to meet your non-negotiable standards, so you're not just dating someone for the sake of sex."

Outlander looked terribly confused.

"Because presumably, you're looking for something more meaningful than a hookup, right?"

He looked even more confused.

"Like Vanessa. Her non-negotiables are no cheating, and he has to spend quality time with her watching romantic comedies or something, and he has to love her unconditionally."

Outlander frowned. "Could she no' just get a dog, then?"

Jenny laughed.

"And you?" he asked as he slid the plate across the bar to her. "Do you really have such a list?"

"God, no," she said with a snort. "That would eliminate a significant portion of my dating pool.

Anyway, it's easy for my friends to have those standards. Vanessa doesn't even date because she's so into her job. She's a lawyer. And Brooke has been dating Grayson for years. He's so besotted, he would clean her floor with a toothbrush. He wouldn't judge her if she ate an entire pizza by herself, which of course, Brooke would never do. Two slices, tops, would be her big pizza binge. Thank you!" She picked up the sandwich. "I also love the dancing."

"What?"

"At weddings. Love the dancing. I mean, how often do you get out and let it all hang out? Did you?"

He blinked.

"Did you dance?"

Outlander leaned back against the counter, his arms crossed over his chest. He looked as if she'd exhausted him. "A wee bit."

If she'd been at a wedding tonight, she would have been on the dance floor, that was for sure. "Nothing more fun than dancing with a bit of an adult beverage buzz. Now that's a non-negotiable for you," she said, and horror of horrors, she followed up that inane comment with a wink. *What in the hell am I doing right now?*

She took a healthy bite of her sandwich as she tried to think of how to rein this all back in. "I took dancing lessons a few years ago," she said in a desperate attempt to turn the comment around. "Ballroom. But I had two left feet. I couldn't do a *paso doble* to save my life. And forget the quick step—my partner said I looked like I was having a seizure. Apparently that was a non-negotiable for him."

God, she wasn't reining anything in, she was rambling and making it worse. Why oh *why* did she always have to talk so much? It was a horrible, ingrained habit of hers—if no one else talked, there was some automatic switch in her that shifted into turbo mode, filling up all the available air with words.

She looked down at her plate. "Well *this* is delicious." She took another big bite of the sandwich. Too big. Her eyes watered. She chewed maniacally and managed to swallow it down. "So delicious!" she said hoarsely. "What's on it?"

"Chutney."

"Chutney! That's different." A little too different for her tastes. "Not familiar. Where do you get it?"

"We make it."

She imagined him and a cute little blonde making whatever the hell was ruining her perfectly good sandwich. The cute little blonde's name was probably something very Scottish, too, like Fiona. They probably wore matching aprons and laughed gaily as they stirred something in a ginormous pot, then fed each other bites of it. She coughed.

"Beer?" He pushed away from the kitchen counter and walked to the fridge.

"Actually, could I have some water?" she asked hoarsely.

He got her a glass of water and set it down before her. "Thank you," she said. He was watching her closely as she drank, probably wondering if he should dial 9-1-1. Jenny put down the glass and forced a smiled. "So whose wedding was it? Yours?" She laughed at her own joke.

His brows dipped.

"Oh, I get it. Too soon in our relationship for me to ask." She laughed again.

Now he just looked horrified.

"Sorry. Dumb joke," she said with an airy wave of her hand. "I know we don't have a relationship…yet." Come on, sometimes, jokes just teed themselves up.

But Outlander didn't think she was as hilarious as she thought she was, and turned to the sink and began to wash things.

Okay, so the sexy guy in a kilt wasn't much of a talker, and clearly he had no sense of humor. "It's so pretty here at Lake Haven. This whole area is beautiful. You know what I like about it? People are so friendly and helpful." That was really more of a guess than actual experience, but whatever.

He turned back to the island and reached for the bag of chips, but before he could do something ridiculous like put them away, Jenny put her hand on the bag to stop him. Her fingers brushed his, and she glanced up into stark green eyes that were boring through her. "Sorry. I'm just really, *really* hungry."

He pulled his hand back from the bag. "And I'm really, *really* knackered."

"Ah. I can take this to my room." She stood up, gathered up the plate and her water as he checked his wristwatch. She resisted the urge to burp as she stuffed the bag of chips under her arm. "Thank you so much, Edan Mackenzie."

He nodded.

God, but he was a tough one. "Has anyone ever told you that you're a very quiet man?"

A vague hint of a smile turned one corner of his mouth, and he arched a brow. "I'd wager a quiet man is the only type of man you've ever met."

Surprised, Jenny laughed. "*Very* funny," she said, nodding. "I've been told I am a woman of many words."

He braced one hand against the island.

"Okay, all right. I know that look," she said. "That is definitely the look of a man who has been kept too long in his apron." She started for the door.

"We're good, then?" he asked through a yawn. "No cake?"

"Surprisingly, no," she said. The waistband of her palazzo pants was so freaking *tight* all of a sudden. "I'll save it for breakfast. What time is breakfast?"

Outlander looked at her like she was crazy, but Jenny was definitely the type of girl who needed to know where her next meal was coming from. "I'm kidding," she said. "But...breakfast will be served, right?"

"No. The inn is closed," he reminded her. "There's a market in East Beach if you need anything."

Jenny had no idea how to get to East Beach, obviously, but she'd figure it out tomorrow. She was suddenly too full and exhausted. "Great. Well, thanks again," she said, and started for the door. When she reached it, she looked back. Outlander was still watching her. Warily. As if he expected she'd make a run at the pantry. "Wi-Fi?" she asked hopefully.

The corner of his mouth rose up so fleetingly that it was possible she'd imagined it. "You canna eat Wi-Fi."

"More's the pity. But I need to email my dad and tell him where I am."

"In the lounge," he said.

"Great. Thanks again, Edan. Good night."

"Good night, then."

She walked out with the vision of a pair of

muscular legs beneath that kilt dancing in her mind's eye.

Of all the gin joints in all the world, she had to walk into his, she thought, in her best Humphrey Bogart accent.

Four

---◆---

The sun slipped through the seam between the drapes to wake Edan the next morning. He groaned, sat up and looked about the spacious and fairly empty master suite he occupied in the turret of the old inn. His kilt was on the chair where he'd tossed it last night. His boxers were hanging off the post at the foot of the bed. His shirt was lying crumpled up on the floor. Sandra, his late aunt's long-time partner, had minded this place for years and would not be happy with his slovenly dispatch of last night.

He hauled himself out of bed. He shoved his hands through his hair and padded naked across the room to the en suite. As he walked by one of the windows, a flash of orange caught his eye. Edan paused. He took a step backward and squinted out the window. That was the motor mouth Jenny, judging by the caramel hair. She was on the first tee of the little 9-hole golf course he'd put in two years ago to attract more guests. She was bent over, her hands and feet on the ground, her hair pooling on the orange mat she'd spread beneath her.

What the bloody hell was she doing? Edan squinted as she suddenly moved one leg back, then rose up, lifting her arms high in the air as she arched her back.

Yoga? On his tee box? What time was it? He glanced around to the clock on the mantel above the hearth. Half past six in the morning. Was she mad? It was a bloody golf course! It was too early for controversy, and yoga on a tee box was definitely his idea of controversy. There was a time and place for everything.

He walked on. Stomping, really, still disconcerted and at odds with the world. Between the wedding and her unexpected arrival, he couldn't seem to find his bearings.

He was being ridiculous, he knew. Yesterday had been a perfect day—the air had been still and crystal clear, the hills around Lake Haven a verdant-green backdrop to the dancing of inebriated, happy adults. The bride and groom had made a beautiful couple.

Edan had known Rosalyn and Hugh since he'd come over from Scotland five years ago to help his aunt with the inn. They'd come a year before him, two ex-patriot Scots who had happened upon work at the inn. At the time, they'd been merely friends. Edan had known almost the moment they'd fallen in love.

Or rather, Audra, his ex-fiancée, had figured it out and had told him.

It had taken Rosalyn and Hugh a while to make

their way to the altar. Edan and Audra were supposed to have been at the altar a full three months before them, but that obviously hadn't happened.

Still, the wedding for Rosalyn and Hugh had been everything Edan could have hoped for them. They were like family to him, especially since he really had none of his own here now. His aunt was gone, his fiancée was gone. All he had was this bloody inn.

The Cassian Inn was an old family estate, left to his American mother and her sister. It had been in the family for generations, but Edan's mother had met a Scot and married him, and had given the inn to Clara. When Edan was nineteen, his mother lost the battle with breast cancer. Fifteen years later, Aunt Clara was diagnosed with the same aggressive form of cancer and had died two years ago.

She'd left her money to Sandra, and the inn to him.

Edan had grown up in Balhaire, a tiny village in the shadow of an old Scottish Highland fortress by the same name. He was the son of a fisherman who was generally out of reach physically and emotionally. Edan's older brother had gone into fishing with his father, and Edan had, too. But when Clara had asked him to come to America and help with the inn just before his thirtieth birthday, he'd lept at the chance. He liked fishing—he just preferred it standing in a trout stream, and not out on the ocean. He did not care for deep-sea commercial fishing at all.

The Cassian Inn was a shadow of what it had once been, as depicted in various old photos around the dining room. Modern finishes and the hacking of grand rooms to create smaller, functional ones, had replaced the Victorian charm. The population around the lake had grown up on the north shore, and even the addition of his golf course had not been enough to bring guests around to the south side of the lake. In the last few years, it had become increasingly difficult to keep the inn booked when just five miles around the bend one might have a room at a the Lake Haven Spa Resort, with upscale spa facilities, boats, and nightly concerts.

Still, for his aunt and Sandra, Edan had done what he could. Rosalyn was the head cook and Hugh the head groundskeeper. Sandra kept the inn clean and the old bachelor Ned manned their little farm. Together, they'd kept the inn lumbering along.

Three years ago, Edan had struck up an online relationship with a girl he'd known in Balhaire. Two years ago, just before Clara's death, Audra had come from Scotland to live with him at the inn. Eight months ago, Audra told Edan she wasn't feeling it anymore. It wasn't the inn, she said. It was him. All him. They weren't on the "same page," whatever page that was. She missed Scotland, she said.

"Then we'll go home," Edan had said instantly. He loved Audra. He had envisioned a quiet life for the two of them, with children eventually, all of them enjoying the relative peace at Lake Haven.

"Aye, Edan, I want to go home. But alone," she'd said with a wince.

There was, of course, more discussion between them. More of his faults had been succinctly outlined for him. He understood Audra had grown bored of life in America, and maybe he'd been a little bored, too. But he'd been blindsided by the news she didn't love him anymore. "I donna know if I ever did, if I am being honest," she'd added, far too casually.

Edan hadn't know what he was to do with that. They had a wedding date. Everyone back home had booked their tickets to the States to see it. He had plans, concrete plans, which started with a wedding.

But she'd packed her wedding dress and left, and Edan had been stuck listening to the happy planning of Rosalyn and Hugh's wedding and listening to break-up songs in his spare time.

To the point he couldn't take it.

To the point he'd decided he ought to be in Scotland. That of course Audra was right, it was too bucolic, too staid. He had come up with the altered plan: He would sell the inn and move back to Scotland and prove to Audra she'd made a mistake. Of course she had. They'd been wild about each other in the beginning. Wires had been crossed, that was all. What was he doing here, anyway?

Yes, Edan had a plan, and he was marching along with it, crossing item after item off the to-do list. He was going back to Scotland to start over.

Today was the last day of his little vacation. The inn would reopen Friday morning for the last bookings, and there was still much work to be done to close the inn down. He planned to reflect on it all with a bit of fishing, perhaps make some mental revisions to the blueprint.

Thank God Rosalyn wasn't here to badger him about it. She said he spent too much time alone. Rosalyn meant well; she loved him like a brother. She and Hugh were concerned about him. *Poor bloke*, they said, *he lost his fiancée. Poor man*, they said, *he rarely speaks.*

That was just his nature. Jenny was right—he was a man of few words. He didn't even know how to come up with more words if he were so inclined.

Audra had complained about it. "Why will you no' *say* something?" she'd said after one heated argument. Edan had never understood what she wanted, exactly. He *did* say things. Just not in long sentences. In fact, now that he was alone, entire days could pass without him uttering a word.

God willing, today would be one of those blessedly quiet days.

Edan dressed, grabbed an apple on his way out, and went down to the shed to gather his tackle and waders. His two Scottish terriers, Wilbur and Boz, trotted along behind him, their snouts to the ground. They followed him to the river's edge past the ruins of an old river mill and a pair of cottage rentals that sat empty.

There was a spot here that he liked very much, a natural outcropping of stones under which trout liked to hide. Old Buggar lived under those rocks. Edan had been trying to catch the brown trout for two years. He'd come dangerously close at the end of last summer, but the bastard had outwitted him time and again. That was disquieting, really, given that a brown trout's brain was the size of an English pea.

Edan affixed his favorite lure to the line, one his father had given to him long ago. "Never lose it, lad," he'd said. "This lure will catch the biggest fish, aye?" That particular day with his father was a vivid memory, and Edan was sentimental about the lure. He'd kept it all these years, but he'd never come close to catching the biggest fish with it.

He'd have to bring that up with his father when he saw him again.

He affixed the lure to his line and waded into the

river. He cast his line. The lure floated softly along the current—until something nibbled at it, jerking it to the right, and Edan began the slow, methodic reeling in.

The line came up empty.

Old Buggar was hungry, was he? He began to swing his arm to cast again, and had just begun to throw when the dogs startled him by barking wildly. He jerked and cast his arm too wide as he tried to catch his balance and the line sailed into a thick hedge of wild bramble bushes on the shore.

"*No!* Bad dog!" a woman shouted.

"*God save me,*" Edan muttered. He turned and scanned the bank. There she was, the woman who couldn't read a sign if it hit her on her nose, the woman who had taken his only bag of crisps, the woman who bent her body in strange ways on his tee box. And now, she'd caused him to toss his line and tangle it in a bush.

He whistled at Wilbur and Boz as he began to slosh toward his tangled line. "Come, you bloody heathens," he shouted to them. The dogs obediently turned away from Jenny and trotted back to him.

"Oh, hey! I didn't see you there!" she called out to him, waving as if he hadn't seen her, either.

Edan reached the bush where his lure had gone. Sharp thorns were thick in the branches. His line was hopelessly caught, the lure dangling in the middle of the stems. Edan reached into a pocket for a knife, cut the line from his pole and set his pole aside. The lure was in the thickest part of the damn bush. Edan carefully reached in. As he worked to free it, grimacing at the nicks of the thorns, he heard feet clomping toward him on the well-worn path beside the river.

Her legs appeared, visible through the stalks of the bramble. "Are you fishing?"

No, he was playing tennis. "I was."

"What are you looking for?"

"My lure."

"What's it doing in there? I don't know that much about fishing, but isn't the lure what the fish tries to get? Maybe you could use worms. I went fishing with my grandfather when I was like, four, and he tried to get me to put a worm on a hook. Disgusting. I never went fishing again."

Edan could almost reach the damn lure and stretched his arm, but his shirt caught on a thorn.

Jenny squatted down. He couldn't see her face through the gap in the bramble shoots, but he could see long, wavy tresses of her hair. "Oh, I get it, you *lost* it. Wow, that's a *lot* of thorns. You're going to hurt yourself, you know. You should leave it. You can buy more at the gas station, I'm sure. They have everything."

He was trying to concentrate and her chatter was not helping.

Her hand suddenly appeared between the shoots of the bush. She had a leather tie and silver bracelet around her slender wrist that momentarily distracted Edan. "I can get it!"

"No—" Edan tried to grab the lure before it slipped, but he was a moment too late—it sank deeper into the bush. And he had a nice long cut across the back of his hand for it.

"Sorry. I thought I had it." She withdrew her hand and began to scratch Wilbur behind the ears. *Wilbur.* The only dog on the face of God's green earth that did not care to have his ears scratched. Not even by Edan, to whom the dog was ridiculously devoted.

Edan was more concerned about the lure. He decided he'd have to fetch a tool to free it. He washed his hands in the water, then stood up, shielding his eyes from the sun as he looked up at Jennifer Turner.

She was standing just above him on the bank, her legs braced apart, her hands on her hips, lightly swaying from side to side as if she were listening to a song in her head. She had changed from the tight-fitting clothing she'd worn to defile his tee box, and was wearing a silky dress that hung to her knees, a sweater over that and, of course, the hiking boots. Her hair, wavy and golden, hung loosely to her waist. She reminded Edan of the flower child of the sixties— natural and free and a wee bit barmy.

"That's really too bad you lost it."

She made him think of sex. Hot, grinding sex.

"Sorry about that. It really sucks because you couldn't have asked for better fishing weather. I've been looking around. This is one gorgeous spot, Mr. Mackenzie. I mean, look at the lake! It's so many colors of blue, and it glitters, like it's studded with crystals. And the hills are so green. I mean, seriously, have you ever seen a more beautiful day?"

No. It would have been perfect for fishing. He swept off his hat and pushed his fingers through his hair, hopefully knocking loose all the thoughts about sex. What he needed was a machete. He couldn't recall seeing one in the tool shed—after all, it wasn't as if they had to hack their way through the bramble for anything.

"Cool boots," she said, nodding, as she checked out his waders. "Very hip. They make your look very outdoorsy."

His waders were not *hip,* they were a functional piece of his favorite pastime, and he *was* outdoorsy.

"I'd be outdoorsy, too, if I lived here," she announced. "But with sunblock. Gotta have that."

He stepped up onto the bank and looked down at her. She smiled up at him. "Is there a reason you've come down to the river, or is this merely a happy coincidence?" he drawled.

"Oh! I almost forgot. Yes, I wanted to ask if there was a bus or something that might take me into East Beach."

"No." He picked up his tackle and his pole and began to walk.

"No? *Really?* I wonder how I'm going to get there," she said, falling in behind him as he strode up the path. Edan glanced back for his dogs—the bloody beasts were trotting along behind Jenny as if they knew her.

"That's the big difference between California and here, you know," she said. "Public transportation. Did I mention that's where I live? I can't remember. Have you been there?"

"No."

"Too bad. Well, anyway, wouldn't it be great if a bus came out here?" She suddenly materialized next to him on the path, her eyes bright as she smiled up at him. "Hey, that's an idea. You could ask whoever runs the buses around here to stop at the top of the road, and then it would be easier for people to find your inn."

Did she honestly think he'd not thought about that? One did not build a golf course without thinking through a thing or two. "No' enough people for it."

"Huh," she said, as if surprised by that. "Then

how does everyone get around?"

"The usual way—car."

"Ah. Is there a driver?"

Edan stopped. "A driver?"

She nodded. "To drive the car. I don't drive. And I obviously don't have a car." She laughed.

"Here's an idea, then—walk."

"Walk!" She laughed again. "I can't *walk* there. It's like five miles! Granted, I am in *great* shape, but I can't just walk five miles there and then five miles back. First, I'd be gone all day, which normally would be okay, but I really need to send that email to my dad, which between you and me is going to take some time to compose. I have to finesse it, you know what I mean?" she asked, wiggling her fingers. "And I *so* want a long bath. A soaking bath. I like to take long baths and read. *Real* books, not an e-reader. I bought this great book at the airport. It's a thriller. The girl gets on the wrong train and ends up in a place she's never been. I'm dying to get into it, but I can't do all that and walk five miles to East Beach and five miles back." She threw up her hands and dropped them again, signifying that was that.

Edan stared at her. "It's *four* miles. No' five."

"It *is*?" she asked, looking at him skeptically. "Well, my point still stands."

Edan carried on to the shed and left her point on the path with her.

She suddenly reappeared beside him. "I guess I *could* walk four miles," she said thoughtfully, following right along. "It's not *that* far."

It was precisely one mile less than the impossible five. Edan put his tackle aside and opened the door of the shed and walked in. He looked around. There was no machete and no pruner.

"I ran a half marathon once," she said.

He glanced over his shoulder; she was leaning against the doorframe, holding a daisy. A bloody daisy. Where had she found that? Ah, of course—from the garden beds they'd passed. So she'd bent down and helped herself, had she? He'd have to keep an eye on her—he wouldn't be the least surprised to see her wearing a wreath on her head made from all his daisies she'd pilfered.

"That's thirteen miles. I was dating this guy who was into running, and it seemed like a healthy thing to do. So I signed up and did it! I had to walk some of it. A *lot* of it. But I did it. FYI, we aren't dating anymore."

"Non-negotiable, was it?" Edan drawled, and passed her in the doorway of the shed on his way to the garden shed a few feet away.

"I think you're getting it," she said. "But that was my choice." She proceeded to explain her brief history of dating a marathon runner as Edan discovered the garden shed was locked. Of course it was—Hugh was very protective of his tools. Bloody key was probably hanging from his belt even now, and Edan wouldn't be the least bit surprised if Hugh had worn the belt on his wedding night.

"And who knows? They might swim across the lake."

"Aye? Pardon?" he said, turning back to the daisy girl. Except that the daisy was gone.

"The bears."

What bloody bears? He hadn't been listening.

"Do you agree with me?"

What was he agreeing to? "Aye," he said

uncertainly.

Her face broke into a brilliant smile. *"Fantastic,"* she said, and her eyes narrowed. "Except that I didn't actually say anything about bears or swimming."

"Did you no'?"

"Nope," she said pertly. "I was just talking about your adorable little dogs. But then I changed them to polar bears just to see if you were listening," she said, pointing to his head and making a circular motion with her finger. "It's a trick I use to see who is paying attention."

"One I would guess you employ quite a lot."

"Ooh, *snarky*," she said, nodding approvingly. "I *like* it."

Aye, she was right. She was a guest at his establishment, the blue streak of words emanating from her lovely mouth notwithstanding, whether he liked it or not. "I apologize. But it's a wee bit hard to listen to all you say, Ms. Turner."

Her big blue eyes widened and Edan thought he'd offended her until she burst into gales of tinkling laughter. "I know, *right*? Don't look so horrified, Edan. It's sure not the first time I've heard that."

Edan had to grudgingly admit to himself that he liked her laugh. It was light and almost lyrical. And he liked the way she had little patches of bird's feet by her eyes when she laughed. "I'll take you to the village," he heard himself say.

She gasped with delight. "You *will*?"

What in God's name had made him say that? "I need a pruner," he said. At least that much was true. "The hardware shop is near a market."

"Thank you so much! I'm just going to grab my wallet!" she said, and skipped off, turning halfway up the path to shout, "Don't leave without me!"

She continued on, and damn it if his bloody beasts for dogs appeared from nowhere to romp after her.

Now, to determine precisely how he could manage this foray into East Beach without being made deaf by her constant chatter.

A half marathon, indeed.

Five

---◆---

Edan Mackenzie, with his dashing good looks and mysterious gaze and taciturn manner, drove a very sporty little car. "Wow," Jenny said as she climbed into the passenger seat. "What is this? A Porsche? A *Jaguar*?" she asked excitedly, looking around.

He looked at her strangely. "It's a Ford."

"Oh."

"Are you ready, then?"

"Let me just buckle in here," Jenny said, and looked around for the seat belt. "You can never be too careful. I read that something like 90 percent of all traffic deaths are caused by people not wearing their seat belts." She had the clip of the belt, and now she was trying to get it into the slot. "That's pretty amazing if you think about it. I mean, with all the drunk drivers on the road, it seems so easy to just—"

He suddenly reached around her, grabbed more of the belt and brought it forward, then batted her hand away from the clip and shoved it in.

"Click it," she finished. Her head was suddenly filled with the scent of Mr. Mackenzie—spicy and musky and *wow,* he smelled so good. She leaned toward him just a little to inhale his scent again—

Edan sank back into the driver's side and started the car, taking off like a shot and speeding around the curves on the road to the main road.

Jenny momentarily forgot how good he smelled so that she could turn all her attention to freaking out, because the man drove like a maniac. He took one corner so fast that the tires squealed—but her squeal was louder.

"Is your brake working, then?" he asked, his eyes on the road.

"Not as well as I would like," she answered truthfully.

In response to that, he goosed it and sent the car moving a little faster.

"I spent way too much time sitting in a car when I was a kid. That's all you do in California—you drive. I mean, if you're not taking the excellent public transportation options. That's what I prefer. Give me a cab or a train or a bus." She braced one hand against the dash and looked at him.

He ignored her. But it would take a lot more than ignoring her to put off Jenny Turner. Edan reminded her a little of her best friend from high school, Caitlyn Emerson. She'd met Caitlyn in ninth grade in chemistry class. Everyone was tasked with choosing a lab partner, and Jenny had noticed no one was choosing Caitlyn. She knew why, they all knew why—Caitlyn had been labeled undesirable. Jenny couldn't remember why any longer—stuck-up, or rude—but there was something about Caitlyn that had seemed vulnerable to her, and Jenny had always been one to rescue people from the fringe. She'd chosen Caitlyn as her lab partner and discovered that the girl was not stuck-up, but painfully shy—debilitatingly so. And when she was confronted with a situation that made her uncomfortable, she came across as aloof and detached.

Sort of like her driver.

Jenny hadn't yet made up her mind about Edan, and she didn't think he was shy like Caitlyn. It was different than that. He was antisocial. But even that didn't seem entirely correct, because she could see something in those beautiful green eyes of his, and what she saw told her that Edan wasn't entirely disinterested. She guessed he probably didn't know what to make of her. Well, get in line, pal—no one ever did. Okay, so she swam in the pool of tree huggers and natural-food enthusiasts, and sometimes, she ignored big signs and she talked too much, that was a given. But none of that made her unlikable or hard to understand.

The faster Edan drove, the more curious Jenny was about him.

"This is a really interesting drive," she said, with both hands against the dash now as they whizzed down the road. "It's moments like this that make me love traveling. I just *love* to go to different places and absorb the culture."

"Riding in a car is no' a culture," he said matter-of-factly.

"Point taken." Her heart was beating wildly as he

took a turn on what felt like two wheels. "Still, *this* ride is very different than any other I've ever had. I didn't know cars could go this fast. You'd think the physics would make it impossible."

He gunned the car onto a bigger road. "On the contrary, it is the physics that make it possible."

She tried to get a glimpse of the speedometer, but she'd have to lean too close to him to see. "People are always in such a hurry, have you noticed? They think a vacation is only a week, and that a week is too long. Trust me, you need at least a month to really get the feel of a place."

He looked at her sharply.

"What?" Jenny asked.

"I canna imagine anyone has so much time to travel about and *absorb*," he said.

"Well, sure, most people don't have the time or money to do it. Honestly, it takes a certain amount of privilege to get away with it. I did it once. I went to Thailand one summer between semesters to study with a yogi there, and I totally absorbed the country. It's in my blood now. Although counter argument— maybe I was there too long. I mean, in the beginning, it was magical. Then I started to notice how hot it was. And the food, forget it—just too spicy. I was actually glad to come home to a good old-fashioned cheeseburger, and I don't even eat red meat. But you know how it is, sometimes, you just gotta get a burger under your belt, right?"

Edan looked at her with the dazed expression she'd seen a few times on him. Sort of like she imagined someone might look at an unidentifiable stain on the countertop as they tried to work out what it was.

They sailed into a small development of businesses and houses, and Edan screeched to a sharp halt in a parking spot.

"Just out of curiosity, how fast were we going?" Jenny asked breathlessly.

He opened the driver's door. "I might have reached seventy on the main road, aye? Here we are, then. I'll fetch you in a half hour from the coffee shop." He pointed to a storefront with the words, *Lakeshore Coffee* painted artfully on the window. He got out, shut the door, and began striding down the road.

"Okay," Jenny said to the empty car, unhooked her seat belt and got out, too.

They were on the main street of the village of East Beach, where storefronts faced the cobbled street. Bright summer flags and flowers hung from street poles, and merchants had pulled their sale items out onto the sidewalk. It was a lovely, charmingly quaint little lakeside village, the sort you'd expect to see in a brochure advertising summer tours.

Cranston's, a small market, was situated next to the coffee shop. Jenny went inside and picked up a basket. For such a small market, it was surprisingly well stocked with whole foods. Fresh produce beneath signs proclaiming it from a local farm was placed near the entrance. Jenny was generally very conscious of her diet, but these days, she was doing more stress eating than worrying about nutrition, and she headed for the aisles in the back. After she'd collected enough snacks to keep her through the Apocalypse—she did not like to leave things to chance—she made her way to the register. "Good morning!" sang the round little woman behind the counter. She had a mop of gray hair and oval glasses perched on her nose that made her brown eyes seem twice their size. "Is this all you'll be needing? We've got a sale on blackberries. They're local, of course."

"Thanks, but this ought to do it," Jenny said.

"Are you with one of the bus tours?" the woman asked as she began to ring up her items. "We usually don't see them for another hour or so."

"Oh, no. I came from the Cassian Inn."

"The Cassian!" the woman said as she scanned a bottle of bubble bath. She turned her magnified brown eyes to Jenny. "I thought the Cassian closed."

"I think it is," Jenny said. "Or closing. Not quite closed, but close enough to closed." She grinned.

"Well, it's no wonder. That place has been limping along since Clara died, and I told my husband when that poor man lost his fiancée that he'd be out of there but quick."

What? Jenny stared at her. Edan's fiancée had *died?* No wonder he was so...churlish.

The woman began to punch numbers into her old cash register. "Yeah, I didn't actually see the closed sign when I arrived last night," Jenny said, which was obviously not true, but she felt compelled to offer an explanation for being there. "The manager was kind enough to let me stay."

The woman stopped punching numbers into the cash register and looked up at Jenny. "Mackenzie?"

"Yep. Edan Mackenzie," Jenny said. "He let me stay because I didn't have anywhere else to go. Other than the bench outside his inn." She smiled sheepishly. "I had an unplanned stop without a back-up plan. But he gave me a room and made me a sandwich."

"Edan Mackenzie made you a sandwich!" The woman gave a bark of disbelief. "Well, maybe he's finally getting over it." She resumed her punching of numbers. "I heard he took it pretty hard. The wedding was planned and everything, and since then, I never see him out and about. He used to come around for coffee, but I don't think he does that anymore. If it weren't for Rosalyn and Hugh, he'd probably rot away up there."

Edan didn't strike Jenny as a man who was going to rot away. He was far more likely to die in a fiery car crash. *Seventy my ass.*

The woman must have realized she was gossiping, because she suddenly said, "Goodness gracious, don't listen to me. My husband says I'm a busybody and he's right. But I did wonder if he was going to close before the Italians came."

"The Italians?"

"There's a few of them that come every year to the Cassian. Brothers, I think. If you ask me, I think they want to marry one of their girls off to someone here and get an anchor in the US. You know how the Italians are."

"No," said Jenny, mystified. "How are the Italians?" Her maternal grandmother was Italian, and Jenny had spent summers at her villa in Italy as a child. She found most Italians quite charming.

"There I go again," the woman said with a laugh and waved a chubby hand before she began to stuff paper bags with Jenny's purchases. "I'm just saying that they are always looking for a place they can turn into an Italian restaurant. That's what they want from Mackenzie, I think. They want to put an Italian restaurant in over there."

That seemed absurdly unlikely and a bit racist. "I love Italian food," Jenny said absently.

"That will be thirty-seven eighty, please."

Jenny fished in her wallet for money and handed it over to the lady. She hoisted two paper bags into her arms and smiled at the woman. "Have a great day," she wished her.

"Oh, I'll have a fine day. You do the same over at the Cassian." The woman punctuated that with a cackle.

Jenny didn't know what she was going to do at the Cassian, honestly. She didn't know what she was doing anywhere. She waved at the woman and stepped outside with her two bags and walked next door to the coffee shop.

Lakeshore Coffee was crowded. Small bistro tables were filled with people drinking out of enormous coffee cups. They were chatting or glued to their laptops. Jenny ordered a bear claw and a cup of coffee, and maneuvered her way out to one of the little bistro tables on the sidewalk.

She had hardly drunk any of the coffee when she spotted Edan. He was just down the street, a plastic shopping bag in one hand. He was speaking to two women. Or rather, they were speaking. She couldn't see his face, but she imagined him standing there, just staring at them with those green eyes, his jaw set. What were they doing? Checking in on him? Asking how he was doing after the death of his fiancée? Maybe they were inviting him over for a kidney pie. One of them looked like a woman who'd done her fair share of baking. Did they eat kidney pie in Scotland, or was that just an English thing? Jenny had tried kidney pie once, at a restaurant in New York. It was god-awful—

Edan suddenly broke away and strode toward her, his walk powerful and strong. He motioned toward the car as he neared her, and for a brief moment, she thought he meant for her to make a run for it. But in the time she took to figure out why they needed to make a run for it, and finish her coffee, he reached her table. He looked down at her bags, then at her bear claw.

"Hi," she said. "I'm not keeping you from your friends, am I?" She looked over his shoulder to where the two women were still standing, their eyes fixed on Edan. Or maybe their eyes were fixed on her—at this distance, Jenny couldn't tell whom exactly they were studying so intently.

"No' friends," he said, ushering her along. "Acquaintances. Come on, then." He reached down and picked up her bags.

Jenny appreciated chivalry, but she hadn't finished her coffee. She stood up, gulped as much coffee as she could, and grabbed her bear claw as she followed him to the car and watched him load her bags into the trunk.

When he closed the trunk, he looked at the bear claw pastry. "Hunger seems to be a constant state with you."

"You have no idea," Jenny muttered.

As they pulled out of the car park and started back the way they'd come, she scrutinized this man who, according to the local grocery store clerk, had lost his fiancée and now wouldn't come out for coffee. It was hard to believe he'd managed to remain free of attachment, knowing what she did about how the female brain operated. He had all the core requisites for the Perfect Match: sexy accent, check. Handsome, check—especially today with that shadow of beard and longish, mussed hair. He needed love, check. Anyone who had suffered the loss of a fiancée needed love. And, last but not least—he had money. Well, she was surmising he did. People who owned inns couldn't be poor, could they?

No matter, she couldn't believe some woman hadn't swooped in to help him with his grief. At least come around to check on him. Just how long had he been hiding away at the Cassian, anyway? And what was this Italian business? She was dying to know the answers to these questions but knew from experience that outright interrogation was not the way to go.

As Edan pulled away from the curb, and she gripped the door to keep her seat as he hit the gas, she asked, as if the thought had just occurred to her, "Just curious, how long have you been in the States?"

"Four hundred years," he said.

Jenny sputtered a laugh. "Well, that's amazing, because you don't look a day over forty."

"Forty!" he exclaimed, and muttered under his breath. "I'm thirty-four, aye?"

"Aye," she said, smiling.

He glanced at her from the corner of her eye before turning a corner. "And you?"

"Twenty-nine," she said.

He looked back to the road.

"So how long have you been here?" she asked.

He slowed to stop at an intersection. "Five years."

"What? That means you arrived when you were twenty-nine, just like me! I mean, *not* like me, but you embarked on a new adventure when you were twenty-nine."

Edan drove on. "Are you embarking on a new adventure, then?"

"Open to interpretation." A lot of interpretation, actually, because she had no clue what she was doing. "Do you ever think about doing something entirely different? A whole new occupation?"

He shrugged as he turned onto the main road and sped up. Jenny put her hand on the dash to keep herself from flying out the window. "No," he said. "I've always known I'd take part in the family business."

"Lucky you. I *still* haven't figured out what I want to do with my life. I've had great ideas in theory. But then, when I pursue them, the actual idea doesn't turn out like I thought. Like minoring in history. I *love* history, and just assumed I'd be a college professor. But there aren't so many of those jobs around, and even if you get one, you have to do all this stuff to get tenure. So then I got into Buddhism."

He seemed startled. "Are those two things related?"

"Nope. But I was interested, and I thought it might lead to something." She snorted. "It didn't. However, it is a very interesting belief system if you're into that sort of thing."

He did not indicate one way or the other.

"Then, I had a job at a plant nursery, which I loved. Except the pay was paltry, and it was really far from my dad—he has Parkinson's and needed me, you know—and I felt dirty all the time, because there is a lot of dirt involved in the plant industry. But I learned a *lot*, and I haven't even mentioned my yearlong stint in premed. I wanted to be a nutritionist. I'm all about whole foods and plant-based diets."

He looked at the half of the giant bear claw in her lap.

"Don't judge me," she said, and took a bite. "So anyway, after that, I was a nanny for the Oosterhausens, and when they moved back to Holland, I figured I'd be good at teaching little kids. So I got a job as an art teacher at a private school."

"You're an artist?" he asked curiously.

"Well, no," Jenny said. "But I *feel* artistic. Anyway, I don't have that job anymore." She took another bite. "Budget cuts," she said through a mouth full of pastry.

Edan was silent. He was probably thinking that her liberal arts degree was perfect for someone who never had the right goals. Or goals that were so vague they required a catchall degree.

"Look, here's the deal—it's about my dad. He's a brilliant scientist," Jenny said, deciding to come clean. She added, *"Really,"* at his skeptical look. "He invented some thing-a-ma-jig for telescopes that NASA bought and it made him insanely rich. But he's also a hoarder, and he's terribly absentminded, which means he does things like leaves the stove on or forgets to take his medicine. All he has is me, and I could never venture too far away from him. I mean, I've traveled some, and I went to college away from him. But he needed me too much, so I've sort of floated around Santa Monica." And then, after several years of being attended almost daily by his devoted daughter and only child, he had inexplicably come up with a girlfriend.

"You're no' there now," Edan said.

"Well, no, because out of the blue, Dad got a girlfriend off Hoarder Tinder. All I know is that my dad, who is a little nutty, and has Parkinson's, and is a hoarder, has better luck than I do when it comes to dating."

Jenny had learned about Cathy at the same time she'd been laid off of her job teaching art to first graders because of budget cuts. Her father had told her not to worry, that he had *plenty* of money.

"Where's your mum?" Edan asked.

"Dead," she said matter-of-factly. "She couldn't take the hoarding." Jenny's mother had once told her the trouble between her and Jenny's father had begun when he got so rich he could buy whatever he wanted. He did. And then he'd filled the house with it. "When I was ten, she took off with a guy on a motorcycle. A few weeks later, he crashed his motorcycle and killed them both."

"Good God," Edan said softly.

Jenny didn't offer that Bethany's opinion was that her mom's death was the reason Jenny never dated the right guy. She'd explained it all a few weeks ago when she'd come out to California for work and they'd met for drinks. "Think about it. You're afraid to commit to anything. A job, a guy...get it?"

"No," Jenny had scoffed, but privately, she wondered it that was true.

"Look. Your mom abandoned you and then she died. Your grandmother died shortly after that. Your dad constantly let you down and then didn't tell you about finding Madge—"

"Her name is Cathy."

"Whatever. Anyway, he was the one person you trusted. Oh, and you had that boyfriend when we were college freshmen who cheated on you, remember?"

"Vividly."

"You have never really found a profession you love, and you don't have to because you're filthy rich and have this father to take care of—"

"I'm not rich. My dad is," Jenny had said, blushing. It was no secret that her dad showered her with money, slipping big sums into her bank account even when she asked him not to.

"Anyway, it's easy to see why you don't want to commit to anything," Bethany had said with a shrug, then had wrapped her lipsticked lips around a straw to sip her cocktail.

Jenny glanced at Edan, who had, predictably, remained silent. But he kept casting strange looks in her direction.

"Why are you looking at me like that?" she asked. "Are you worried about my bill?" She flicked her wrist. "Don't worry—I have rivers of money."

"I think you're a wee bit mad," he said, and sounded, Jenny thought, a little too concerned.

"No! It's just that sometimes, life is so lovely it's hard to know where to start, right? It's not like I don't understand that I have a bad work history. But I haven't figured out what I want from life yet. I thought I'd be taking care of my dad forever, but he...well, he clearly doesn't need me quite like I thought."

Edan glanced out the driver window and added, "Sorry about that."

His sudden spurt of empathy surprised her. "*Thank* you." Her friends never said sorry about her dad—they thought Jenny ought to be glad he had a girlfriend. She was, but there was more to it than that. She was sad about it. Inexplicably sad. "Life goes on, right?"

"Aye. That it does," he said with a sigh.

That's what her father had said. *"Life goes on, Jenny. You have to live your life now."*

"I am going to get a job, you know," she said. "I haven't exactly landed on what it is just yet, but I'm thinking—" Jenny was startled by the ring of her phone. "Oh, that's mine." She dug it out of her pocket and looked at the number. God, it was Bethany. She punched it silent.

It rang again.

"You should answer it," he said.

"It's a friend."

"I donna mind," he assured her. Probably so she'd stop talking to him—this was not Jenny's first rodeo. "Okay," she said, picking up the phone, as the ring seemed to grow louder. "But if you hear some yelling, don't be alarmed."

"What?"

"Hello?" Jenny said into the phone.

"Turner Tots! It's Bethany. What's up?"

"Umm...not much."

"Not much? Not anything you want to mention to a friend? Maybe about how you and Doofus broke up?"

Jenny glanced sidelong at Edan. His interest had expired; he was watching the road ahead of him, his expression like someone who was miles from where they actually were. "Well hello, Bethany," she said. "Can you turn it down a notch or two? And how do you know about that?"

"No, I cannot turn it down a notch or two. I just got a call from Bozo, because he lost your number in some weird phone accident where he could only see some numbers, not all of them, I don't know, it made

no sense, but anyway, are you okay?"

"I'm fine. What did he want?"

"Money, probably. I refused to give him your number. Where *are* you?"

"At Lake Haven."

"East Beach?" Bethany asked.

"Nope. Other side of the lake," she said, glancing from the corner of her eye at Edan. "A darling inn." It *was* darling. It was so unique.

"What happened? What did that asshole do?"

"Now is not a good time," Jenny said, and to Edan, she rolled her eyes and made a whirling motion at her head to indicate Bethany was nuts.

"Why not? What are you doing? Jesus, Jenny, go to Vanessa's."

"I'm fine!" Jenny insisted. "I don't need to go anywhere. I mean, not at this precise moment. It happens to be very beautiful here. And peaceful."

"Is it like, a camp?"

"No!"

"Please promise you're not going to go off and try and camp by yourself."

Jenny was not going to do that, but she didn't like the insinuation that she was somehow incapable. At least Misty Pachenko had taught her how to pitch a tent before fucking Devin. "I really like it here. It's where I want to be right now. I have a lot to think about."

"Jen-*ny*," Bethany said. "This is what you always do! You jump from frying pans to fires."

Jenny's pulse began to quicken. She was getting angry. She tried to shift around in the passenger seat so that Edan couldn't see her face. "Please explain to me *why*, when I do something different than any of you would do, that the assumption is that something is wrong with *me*? Different strokes, baby."

"Well here's the big difference," Bethany said. "We all have *jobs*. Listen, it's your life to live and all that, but come on, Jen, you can't live like this forever. We say something because we care. You can't live like a gypsy."

Jenny blinked. Her heart leapt with indignation. "Since when did everyone become my mother?" she exclaimed, forgetting Edan. "I am fully in charge of my life, Bethany. I am mindful and centered and I know what I'm doing."

"No you don't," Bethany said. "You yourself have said you don't know what you're doing with your life. Don't make me come and get you."

"Please. You wouldn't leave your job for a moment or the whole telecom industry will fall apart, remember?"

Bethany hesitated at the truth in that statement. "I didn't say I was coming tomorrow. Maybe Monday."

"*Ha*," Jenny said triumphantly. "I may not be here Monday."

"Why? Where are you going?"

"I don't know!" Jenny shouted. "Life's a journey, Bethany, and I'm on the train! I am *living*! I don't know where I will go from here just yet, but I promise, you will be among the first to know." She glanced at Edan. She had to hand it to him—he was smooth. His expression was completely inscrutable.

"Look, I have to go," Bethany said. "Call me when you can talk and tell me what happened. We'll help you make a plan."

"I don't need you to help me make a plan," Jenny snapped. "I'll call you later."

"Fine. Call me," Bethany said curtly, and hung up.

That was one thing that could be said for the four of them. No matter how mad they got at each other, anger never got in the way of their friendship.

She looked at Edan from the corner of her eye. The sudden silence felt oppressive. "I'm sorry you had to hear that," she said with a wince.

"No' my business."

"My friends think they know everything."

"It's no' necessary—"

"I mean, yes, she has a point, I do tend to flit from one thing to another, but that doesn't mean it's *wrong*—"

"You need no' explain."

"I *like* having different experiences. I *like* searching for my place." No she didn't. She hated not knowing what her place was in this world.

Edan said nothing. And surprisingly, neither did Jenny for the rest of the way to the Cassian Inn. When he stopped the car, Edan wordlessly got out.

Jenny sighed and got out, too. He was already at the trunk and handed her the bags of groceries. "Do you need help getting them in, then?"

"No, no, I can get it. Thanks for the ride," she said, and smiled.

"Welcome."

She would be so relieved if he would just smile, even a little. But he merely looked at her, as if he was waiting for her to speak. "Okay. Well. I've got it from here. I'm just going to go inside and contemplate the universe for a bit. And I know you're dying to get down to the river and cut down that bush and get the thing that fell off your fishing pole."

"It didna fall off," he reminded her. "And it's a lure."

"Whatever," she said airily.

He walked with her to the door of the inn and held it open for her. Jenny maneuvered in with her two bags of groceries, then turned around to thank him— but Outlander had already closed the door. She heard his car a moment later move off the drive.

Dammit. She liked that silent Scotsman. But she was pretty sure the feeling was not mutual.

Six

Life is so lovely it's hard to know where to start.

That was quite possibly the barmiest thing Edan had ever heard.

But surprisingly erudite.

He was determined to go back to Scotland. He intended to fix this rift between him and Audra. It was fixable, he was certain of it. But did he really want to join his father and brother in the family deep-sea fishing business? Days on end of nothing but endless sea and waves that could roil the sturdiest of constitutions? Was that really the right place to start? But what else might he do? All he'd ever done was that and help Aunt Clara run her inn.

With his fishing pole and his pruners, his tackle and his dogs, Edan walked up the hill to the old family graveyard. He went in through the rusty gate and stood a moment, soaking in the sun and quiet, the view of the lake and beyond. It was as lovely a final resting place as existed in the world, he supposed, and Aunt Clara had wanted to be buried here.

As Wilbur and Boz began to sniff around the markers, Edan brushed some leaves from Clara's headstone. *Here lies Clara Catherine Monroe, Beloved Daughter, Sister, Aunt...*

She had definitely been beloved. She'd been ten years younger than Edan's mother, and she'd always felt more like a cousin or sister than aunt to him. He'd loved her like a sister, certainly. He'd trusted her explicitly, had found her easy to talk to. And she'd always given him good advice.

He'd started coming up here to her grave when Audra left him.

He squatted down and pulled a few weeds that had sprung up at the base of the headstone. "No rain for a week," he said aloud. "It's been beastly hot." He didn't know why he always started with the weather. It wasn't as if Aunt Clara had ever been particularly interested in weather and she certainly wasn't now.

He settled back on his heels and said, "I've a guest. The inn is closed, aye, but I discovered her after Rosalyn and Hugh's wedding Sunday evening. She appeared on the doorstep like a bloody orphan and I couldna turn her away." He pulled another weed. "She's a barmy lass," he said. "It's always an American off on some daft adventure, is it no'? Remember the bloke with the glasses? The one who stayed in his room for a week?" Edan shook his head—he still wasn't convinced that strange young man hadn't been plotting something awful in his room that week. "The lass had nowhere else to go."

He sighed, and picked another weed.

"You'd no' believe how she talks, Clara. She havers on without as much as a breath. I canna begin to recall all she's said, and I'll be damned if I know what to make of it." He looked curiously at the headstone. "Did Audra talk so much? I canna remember precisely. Did you?" It seemed so odd to him that characteristics of people he loved that were once so vivid turn to monochrome with time.

He turned his head and squinted as he looked out over the lake. "She's pretty," he blurted. "The lass, I mean. I like her hair. Pretty blue eyes, too." He ran a hand over his crown. "And a proper bonny smile. But she's bloody *barmy*," he said again with a shake of his head.

Boz wandered over and stuck his muzzle under Edan's hand, wanting to be petted. Edan absently stroked the dog's ears, then finally stood up. He gazed down at Aunt Clara's headstone. If she were here, she'd tell him to get on with it. To stop moping, to look forward. She'd tell him that Audra ended it between them, and there was no point in wishing it weren't so. That he had a lot of life ahead of him, far too much life to waste time crying about a breakup.

Life is so lovely it's hard to know where to start.

He did not want to debate with Clara's ghost. "I'm going fishing," he announced, and picked up his things, and walked out the old iron gate and down to the lake.

On the edge of the lake, Edan chopped down the blasted bramble bush and managed to retrieve his lure. He'd come so close to losing it that he opted for a different lure for afternoon fishing. That lure didn't work on Old Bugger, but he did manage to catch two small trout. Fresh fish would be nice on the grill tonight. He'd clean up, do some paperwork, and then fire the grill. Tomorrow, Rosalyn and Hugh would return, the inn would reopen, and by the weekend, the inn would receive the last bookings. In two weeks, it would be shuttered. Put on the market. Rosalyn and Hugh were moving to the city. Sandra, who had been Clara's partner for twenty years, was going to live with her sister in Buffalo. Ned was retiring to East Beach.

Edan whistled for his dogs and trudged home with his two fish. The inn, a massive Victorian mansion built in the style of the American monied upper class before the stock market crash, had been brought into the twenty-first century with a few additions. He had private living quarters, a terrace with a barbecue grill, and a renovated kitchen. It was his personal kitchen, rarely used, but gleaming with promise.

Edan cleaned the fish, fed his dogs, and showered. He went over some paperwork that needed his immediate attention. By the time he'd finished, it was early evening. On the terrace, he fired the grill, brought out his fish, and helped himself to whisky as the fillets slow cooked.

It was a nice evening, cool and still. Edan was sitting on one of the padded chairs, his head back, his eyes closed. He was tired—he'd been running for weeks with the work of following his plan to close down the inn and put it up for sale. The work had caught up to him. He put aside his whisky, sank deeper into that chair.

But something felt off. He opened his eyes—and jumped to his feet.

"Sorry! I didn't want to disturb you. You looked like you were sleeping. Were you sleeping?"

It was *her* again. What was she doing here? How had she managed to wander back into his private grounds? And why was she holding lettuce and a cucumber?

"You're probably wondering what I am doing," she said, as if reading his mind.

Edan stared at her.

"I rang the little bell, but no one came."

"Aye. For as we've previously established, the inn is *closed.*"

"See? That's the problem. I hate to bother you, but I didn't know what else

to do. I need a bowl. And a knife," she said, and held out her lettuce and cucumber. "And there is no one to ask at the front desk."

Edan looked at her produce.

The lass looked at the grill. "*Something* smells delicious."

The fish, for God's sake. Edan lunged toward the grill. He quickly turned the filets as she crowded in next to him to have a look. "Did you catch those today? They smell so good! What kind of seasoning did you use?"

He closed the grill and glared down at her.

She was wearing a long skirt and a loose, boxy sweater that swung around her hips. She'd braided her hair and the tail of it hung over her shoulder. She looked fresh. Full of spirit. She smiled at him with those brilliant blue eyes and held up her lettuce and cucumber again. "I could make enough for two, you know."

Edan folded his arms. "Are you seriously offering

a head of lettuce in exchange for fish I labored to catch?"

"Hear me out. It's me and this lettuce, and you've surely figured out by now that I like my three squares. I'm not likely to take no for an answer."

"You brought two bags of food from East Beach only a few hours ago," he reminded her.

"Well, yeah, but not *dinner*," she said, as if between the two of them, he was the one who was absurd.

He pondered her. A private dinner with a guest was not a good idea, exactly, but really where was the harm? He wouldn't mind the company. Or at least he *hoped* he wouldn't mind the company after it was all said and done. "How are you at washing up?" he asked.

"Hmm." She titled her head to one side. "Do you want the politically correct answer, or the truth?"

Edan couldn't suppress a small smile. "The truth."

"So-so," she admitted. "But I give it 110 percent. Does that count?"

"No' really," he said. "But I suppose it will have to do if I want your lettuce, aye?"

She gasped with delight. "Thank you *so much*," she said, clasping her cucumber to her breast. "You won't believe this, but I'm—"

"Starving," he finished for her with another wee smile, and gestured toward the kitchen.

She followed him inside, stopped in the middle of the room and looked around her. "Wow," she said. "Just *wow*. So *this* is what a mansion's kitchen looks like."

"It's what my kitchen looks like. This is the

private residence."

"I thought it would be more primitive. You know, very Victorian with a lot of giant cast-iron kettles hanging everywhere." She looked at him sidelong. "And when I say primitive, of course by that I mean charming."

"Of course," he said dubiously.

"This is gorgeous!" she said again, turning a slow circle as she looked around. "I like a family style kitchen."

He'd had little to do with the styling of it. Audra had put a farm table in the middle of the room with six chairs around it. There was a nice sized fireplace at one end that was original to the house. And there was a very large pantry, which had once contained all the dishes for a very large household. It seemed strange to Edan now, given that he really had no need for a kitchen this size, and if he did, then there was a perfectly serviceable one in the main part of the inn.

"If I had a kitchen like this, I'd be a better cook," Jenny declared. "I love the sink."

He glanced at the farm sink. "I put that in. The plumbing, too. And the stove," he added idly. He'd done more work than he gave himself credit for. He dipped down to one of the lower cabinets and retrieved a bowl, then set it next to a cutting board.

"So you're a handyman *and* a fisherman," Jenny said cheerfully. She joined him at the kitchen island and set her produce on the cutting board. Edan reached around her to fetch a knife from the butcher's block. His arm brushed against the silky sleeve of her sweater. She was so close that he caught the sweet scent of her hair, too, and it reminded him of flowers in a spring garden. Frankly, it reminded him of females in general, with soft skin and slender limbs, and…

What in bloody hell am I thinking?

A ripple of consternation slipped through him. He was going home to try and make it work with Audra at the end of the month. He put the knife on the cutting board. "Here you are, then. I'll have a look at the trout."

Outside, Edan finished off the whisky he'd been drinking when she showed up. The warmth of the liquor settled him—he quit thinking about fragrant hair and shapely legs, and brought the fish inside on a plank.

Jenny had found the aprons hanging on a hook and had donned one, and was busily chopping up her cucumber at the kitchen island. But the sight of her was slightly jarring—he was not accustomed to seeing anyone else in his kitchen besides Audra—and for a moment, it was almost like seeing her ghost. That was precisely where Audra would stand to prepare food, her blonde hair falling over her brow. Humming. Audra was always humming.

He remembered that now with a twinge of sorrow. Something had been lost between them, a very long time ago.

Jenny leaned over the kitchen island to get a look at the trout. "Well now, that looks delicious. I don't suppose you have any wine to go with it?"

"All civilized men have wine to go with fish. What sort of wine would you like, lass?"

She stopped chopping and gave him a pointed look. "*Jenny*," she said, and smiled sweetly. "My name is Jenny. I know you know that, but I am reminding you in case it slipped your mind now that we're hanging out."

"Now that we're…? We're no' hanging out," Edan said instantly, quite sure he'd never uttered those words in his life, and quite sure this was not *that*.

"Yes we are," she said with great assurance. "A man doesn't offer to take a woman to town and then invite her in for dinner if they aren't hanging out."

He gaped at her. "How have you managed to finagle your way into a ride and invite yourself in for dinner and somehow convince yourself it was the other way around?"

"Well, whatever you want to call it, we keep ending up together—"

"*We* donna end up together. You keep appearing," he said, gesturing in the direction of the terrace.

"Yes, and *you* keep calling me lass. Not that I'm opposed to that," she said. "I actually like the way it sounds. *Lass*. I get a shivery feeling when you say it. It's kind of a turn-on."

Edan raised his brows. What the hell was she talking about now?

"Hey," she said, gesturing with her knife, "don't you think it's interesting, all the little things that are a turn-on to people? Like your accent, or the way you call me lass. Hands are a turn-on, too," she said, and held up her hand.

Edan looked at his.

"See?" she said, wiggling her fingers at him. "*Hands.*"

"Who *are* you?"

"I told you. Jenny. Don't forget it." She winked.

"I think there is verra little chance I shall ever forget it," he said in all sincerity.

Jenny laughed, and her eyes had a mischievous little shine to them. He put the trout down. "All right, then. What sort of wine would you like, *Jenny?*" he asked, articulating her name.

Her lips curved into a pert grin. "White, please, *Edan.* Is it all right if I call you Edan? I know I have and I didn't ask you before, but you said most people call you Mr. Mackenzie, which, let's be honest, does not feel right, especially since, you know, we have this thing going." She gestured between them with a knife. "We're like, two peas in a pod."

"We're no'," he countered.

"But we are! We both embarked on a new adventure at the age of twenty-nine. We're both at Lake Haven. We're both sort of drifting."

"*Drifting?*"

"And there is no way you're an Ed." She popped a bit of cucumber into her mouth. "So I'll just call you Edan," she said, and resumed her chopping.

Edan had been boxed into speechlessness. She was so wildly illogical that it was oddly and inexplicably charming. He didn't care what she called him, really, and if he were honest, he'd admit to himself that he liked the way she said his name. It sounded flat and smooth and a wee bit off the mark when she said it.

What is happening? Since when had he given so much thought to what people called him? Or how his name sounded?

Edan retreated to the wine cellar, his thoughts swirling around what she'd said. She was right—he hadn't said her name. Up until this point, it hadn't seemed necessary. But he'd had ample opportunity to say it—for example, *Jenny, go home.* Frankly, what floated unappealingly in his belly was that in saying her name he felt absurdly disloyal to Audra.

Well, that was sheer lunacy for you. There was no reason he should feel remotely disloyal to a woman who had announced she didn't love him and had left him. But he did a wee bit, because he thought he and Audra could work things out, and in some dusty corner of his soul, saying Jenny's name was different somehow. It was a new whisper in his heart.

Whatever ridiculous thoughts were rumbling about in him, Edan couldn't sort it out now, especially not with the prospect of dinner before him.

He selected a bottle and returned to the kitchen.

Jenny had finished tossing the lettuce and cucumber salad, which she announced with a cheerful, "*Ta-da!* Do you have any olive oil?"

Edan fetched her the oil, poured the wine, then grabbed plates, silverware, and napkins. They sat at the old farm table across from each other. Generally, Wilbur and Boz were at his feet, but tonight, of course, they were at hers.

Jenny made a swooning noise as she tasted the fish. "I'm in heaven. It's *delicious.* What did you do to it?"

"Caught it."

She giggled. "I swear, I never had trout this good in California." She sipped her wine. "Actually, I may have never had trout in California. Have you ever been to Catalina? I had the *best* fish there. You would never guess what kind—guess."

"I donna know."

"Guess!"

"Shark."

"*Eel!*" she all but shrieked. "Did you know you

can *eat* eel? Like, who would want to? Who was the first person to see an eel and think, yeah, I'll have some of *that*?" She shivered.

She continued to chatter through the meal, filling him in on all the strange things she'd ever eaten or seen. Edan didn't have to say much. He'd never been good at small talk, and thankfully, Jenny seemed perfectly content to do all the talking.

But he was smiling.

Jenny moved from strange bites to tales of the camping she'd done before she was, as she had said, suddenly single. Camping on the beach sounded bloody awful. The Catskills sounded lovely. The truth was that Edan hadn't seen much of the States—he'd been so caught up in the inn since arriving a few years ago that there had never seemed time.

Jenny was clearly enchanted with East Beach and Lake Haven. "Such a *beautiful* place," she said for the second time that day. "I've never seen so many trees. So many different shades of green.

"Aye."

Jenny put down her fork. "That's all? *Aye?* But it's so pretty."

Edan shrugged. "I'm from Scotland."

"Oh, so once you've seen Scotland, nothing else compares?" she teased him.

"Something like that, aye. Have you ever been?"

"Nope."

"Then I'll show you." He picked up their plates and took them to the kitchen island, then returned to the table with his laptop. He sat on the same side of the table with Jenny. "My brother is an amateur photographer," he said as he clicked on to his brother's Facebook page. He hadn't visited that page in a couple of weeks—Bran didn't post consistently. But Bran had posted a new crop of photos in the last few days. Photos of the gold and green hills around Balhaire, the small village where Edan had been raised, and the old castle fortress on the hill. Sunsets that glistened red and gold and yellow on the water. The blue and purple mists of the morning.

Jenny studied each photo, exclaiming at the beauty, peppering him with questions. But as Edan scrolled down his brother's page, he noticed a picture someone else had posted and tagged to Bran. The picture was of several people outside the Black Thistle Pub, probably fifteen of them, Edan's father and brother included. They were lifting their mugs of ale in a cheer of some sort. But what caught Edan's eye was Audra. She was in the back of the group with Sean McCaul, a friend of his. And while everyone else toasting whoever had taken the picture, Audra was kissing Sean.

Jenny was talking exuberantly, but Edan was too stunned to hear her. *Since when?* Was it really so surprising? The logical side of him knew that she'd made a clean break from him. But the emotional side of him somehow remained convinced that she didn't mean it. That she'd wanted to go home, and when he followed her, she'd have a change of heart.

The emotional side of him was a bloody idiot.

"It's gorgeous," Jenny said, and closed the lid of his laptop. "All right, Scotland and America. Where else have you been?" she asked.

He looked blankly into her very blue sparkling eyes. "Ah..." He and Audra had gone to the Canary Islands for a week before coming to the States. Good God, had it really been that long since he'd taken time for himself?

"Oh my God, you really *are* a hermit," she said gaily when he didn't answer.

"I'm no' a hermit—"

"You say tomato, I say recluse. Where would you go if you could pack a bag and leave tomorrow?"

"Scotland, aye? I'm going there at the end of the month."

"Yes, but where would you go on *vacation*?"

"Scotland," he said again, hardly thinking.

"*Ai yi yi*," she said with an exaggerated roll of her eyes. "Okay, so what are you going to do there?"

"Fish," he said absently.

"*Fish!*" she repeated. "Don't say more, because the excitement could stop my heart. You're going all the way to Scotland to fish?"

"What else would you have me do?" he asked a little curtly. He had a sudden image of Audra sitting precisely where Jenny was now. "*You're so tiresome, Edan. You're stuck on this bloody loch, living the life of an old man.*"

"I don't know. You could do one of those Highland games. Be a Highlander like Outlander!" she said with delight.

"I'm no' a Highlander," he said a little curtly.

"We're all something," she said. She had twisted about in her chair to face him, clearly enjoying the conversation.

"Aye, you're a gadabout."

She tipped her head back with a shout of laughter. "*Gadabout*! That's so old-fashioned!"

"And you're bloody well aimless," he added.

Jenny's smile faded a little, and he instantly felt awful for having said it. She wasn't aimless. He was astute enough to know he was really lashing out at Audra.

"So I've been told," she said with a weary sigh. "Today, as a matter of fact." She lifted her wineglass, holding it up in a mock toast. "Touché, Mr. Mackenzie. Although I'd like to suggest I'm more undecided than I am aimless. I aim for lots of things—I just never hit what I'm looking for." She clinked her glass against his.

"I'm sorry, Jenny," he said. "That was uncalled for. I didna mean it."

"Don't be sorry. I know who I am and I'm okay with it, and not everyone can say that, can they?" she asked, her brows dipping slightly over her glittering blue eyes.

"No," he admitted.

"Seriously, why aren't you with someone, Edan? You seem like the kind of guy who should be with someone."

The question startled him. He looked around the kitchen, half expecting some camera crew to leap out and declare this some sort of prank. When none did, he said, "Where did that come from?"

"From curiosity. It's a reasonable question," she said. "You're a catch."

He thought he could feel himself blushing, amazingly enough. "I'm no' a *catch*—"

"You are."

Edan stared at her, debating how much to say. "I should have been married three months ago, but it was called off."

"Three *months*?" Jenny put down her wineglass. "I am so, so sorry, Edan. I didn't realize she'd died so recently."

"Died," he repeated, his brows knitting in confusion. "What are you talking about?"

"Your fiancée. I heard in East Beach that you'd lost your fiancée."

Edan didn't know what to say. "You were in East Beach for a half hour at most, and somehow, my fiancée came up?"

"The clerk at the market asked where I was staying and... Well, we had a chat."

Edan could just bet they did. He rubbed his face and sighed. "She didna die, lass. She left."

"*Oh.* She said you lost her—"

"Aye, I lost her to Scotland. She's gone, but no' dead. Quite alive, it would seem."

"I'm so sorry," she said again.

He shrugged. What was there to say?

"But why?" she asked. "Why would she leave this beautiful place and her handsome fiance?"

He smiled self-consciously. "She said it bored her. I suppose I did, too."

Jenny stared at him, as if trying to work out which part of him was boring.

"Why aren't you with someone, then?" he asked her, unwilling to say more about himself. Or face the possibility that Audra might be right about him.

"Easy," she said with a breezy flick of her wrist, "men don't like me like that. I mean, I do okay—but let's just say I spend a lot of time in the friend zone. Not that I haven't had boyfriends," she hastened to assure him. "They just never last long."

That seemed mad to him. What healthy man wouldn't want a very pretty, if slighty mad lass?

She laughed at his expression. "Don't look so shocked. It happens all the time, doesn't it? You meet some guy or girl and you think they're great, and then after the glow wears off, and a few months pass and you're like, *anh*," she said with a dismissive shrug of one shoulder. "Or, I'll meet a nice guy, and we'll hang out as friends, and then I'll start to believe that maybe there could be more between us, and then he'll blow it by saying, 'Hey, is your friend Vanessa seeing anyone?'"

She laughed again, but the laugh wasn't as bright as before. It sounded almost bitter.

"Did you no' just break up with someone?" Edan asked, confused. "Did you no' say you were suddenly single?"

"I did. I am. That guy was bad news and I'm mad at myself because I knew it going in." She leaned forward and looked into her wineglass, and for a moment, he thought perhaps she'd spotted a bit of cork floating about. "We were on this *journey* together," she said quietly, making air quotes. "But the more I was with him, the more I was like, *ugh.* And then, to top it off, I caught him cheating. Like totally *in* the act." She shuddered.

Her boyfriend sounded like the worst sort of bloke. Edan thought of Audra with Sean and felt a bit of a churn in his belly. Audra wasn't cheating, but he supposed it was never easy to see someone you'd been with locking lips with someone else. "That sucks," he said.

"Yep," she said. "But I'm not too sad about it. It was for the best. Devin was more of a stop gap, really."

"What does that mean, a stop gap?"

"I don't know," she said with a bit of a shrug. "I guess after I got laid off, and my dad announced he didn't need me anymore, I didn't really have any place to go, you know? Devin was the only one with a tangible offer."

He glanced down, absorbing that. She was starting to make more sense to him. "I'll be totally honest, Edan—I don't really know what I'm doing," she admitted. "I don't know where I want to go or what I want to do. I need a plan, and I don't have one yet. All I know is that I love it here. It's so peaceful and calm and away from all that," she said, gesturing to his door, as if *that* was waiting for her outside. She swiped up her wineglass and drained it, put it down and said, "That's my story. What's yours?"

"My story is that I have a plan," he said. The last thing Edan wanted to do right now with the day's last bit of light shining in through the window was to talk or think about Audra. He shrugged. "I'm closing the inn and putting it on the market, then heading home." He suddenly stood up, unwilling to discuss the reasons of his decision. "Might I offer you anything else? Crisps?"

"Curly fries?"

He frowned.

"Kidding! Sort of." She stood up, too, and carried their glasses into the kitchen. The dogs, understanding there would be no scraps to fall off the table now, trotted out of the room.

"So this place is lonely for you," she said.

He wouldn't call it lonely, precisely. What he felt was distance—from the world. From life. "It's fine," he said, and turned on the water at the sink.

"Stand aside, captain. I'll do cleanup. That was the deal."

"I meant it as a joke. I'll do it."

She took the sponge from his hand. "Come on, you have to let me do the dishes," she insisted. "You've fed me twice now. The least I can do is scrub your plates."

"There no' enough plates to make up for giving you a room," he pointed out, and took the sponge back from her. She was standing so close that he could see flecks of gray in her crystal-blue irises. "You'll be wanting to get back to something pressing, I suspect. A bath and a book. A real book. No e-reader for you."

Her lips curved up in a smile of pure pleasure. "You *get* me." She continued to hold his gaze, her smile soft. She had such bonny, mesmerizing eyes—

She suddenly rose up on her toes and before Edan understood what she intended, she kissed him. She kissed him with lips as soft as butter, her fingers silk on the stubble of his face. It was a sweet kiss, hardly a kiss at all, really, and yet Edan's body responded like a bomb had detonated in him. He felt himself tumbling hard and fast down a path of desire, and alarmed, he lifted his head, his eyes locked with hers.

She looked so fucking alluring now, with the blush in her cheeks and her wet lips. She also looked stunned. *She* was stunned? He was floating somewhere between earth and God knew what.

"I shouldn't have done that," she said breathlessly, as if she'd read his mind. "I have no idea what got into me. I promise, I don't go around kissing men willy-nilly—" She didn't finish her thought because she grabbed the collar of his shirt and yanked him closer. Wine sloshed out of a glass he was holding and onto his pants leg as she kissed him again. Only this time, she kissed him so violently that he stumbled back against the kitchen counter, and Jenny came with him, her body pressed against his, her arms around his neck. He somehow managed to put one glass down and caught her around the waist. His mind shouted at him to push her away, but his body held onto her, anchoring her there, pressing against the length of her. Jenny nipped at his lips, swept her tongue into his mouth, shoved her fingers into his hair.

She bloody well *kissed* him.

Edan was quickly and dangerously aroused. It was as if a sleeping giant had been awakened, and his body was hardening with want. He swept his hand up to her breast, filled his palm with it, and Jenny moaned.

That small moan jolted Edan back to his senses. What the hell was he doing? He suddenly shifted back from her—which meant quite a backbend, as they were crammed up against the kitchen counter.

Jenny blinked with surprise at the abrupt end of the kiss. She stepped back and stared at him, wide-eyed, as she slowly ran the pad of her thumb across her lower lip. "That was *crazy*," she said in a whisper. "I can't believe I did that. Edan, I don't know what to say. I honestly have no excuse. I mean, you looked like you could use a kiss, but that gives me no right to just *do* it without your consent. I'm a *huge* advocate of consent. I had this friend that—"

"Jenny," he said, before she could launch into a story that would make no sense to him.

"Right. I apologize."

The thing was, she didn't look apologetic. She looked like she was only moments away from ripping his clothes off, and Edan was only moments away from allowing it. He cleared his throat. "I think you best go back to your room, aye?"

She put her hands on her hips. Her gaze fell to his mouth. "You're probably right," she said. But she didn't move. Her eyes were glistening with what he read as desire. "I do want to get an early start tomorrow," she muttered, as if trying to convince herself.

"Leaving Lake Haven?" he asked evenly.

"Don't know," she said to his mouth. "You'll have to wait until tomorrow to find out." She tossed her braid over her shoulder like she was on a runway and suddenly started for the door.

Edan followed her out onto the terrace.

She paused and looked up at the sunset. "Yep, it's stunningly beautiful here. Not Scotland beautiful, maybe. But beautiful all the same."

"Aye," he said. But he was looking at her.

She glanced up at him. "Listen—"

He quickly held up a hand to stop her before she could say anything.

Of course that didn't stop her from saying more. "I can be really impulsive, obviously. I guess that's not exactly news, but sometimes, I get a little carried away. I'm just saying—"

"We're good," he said.

Jenny smiled. She teasingly shoved his shoulder. "Okay, if you say so." She walked down the steps to the grass. "Oh, by the way, is the restaurant opening tomorrow?"

She was the most unusual woman. Edan was a little dazzled by the kiss and really didn't know what to say. He shoved his hands into his pockets. "Do you think you might have a tapeworm?"

Jenny laughed gaily. She had a beautiful spirit to match her beautiful smile. "I probably should get that checked out." She picked up the sides of her skirt, held them out, and curtsied. "Thank you for a lovely evening, Mr. Mackenzie," she said in an awful British accent. "See you," she said, and fluttered her fingers at him before tottering off. She trailed her fingers lazily across the backs of his lawn chairs, and as she walked along, the caramel-colored braid of hair swung above her hips.

Edan stood there watching her walk away, his hands still deep in his pockets, that kiss still thrumming through his body. When she'd disappeared into the shadows of dusk, he walked to the edge of the terrace and looked out over the golf course and the lake beyond. He saw horses grazing in a fenced field, the blurry shapes of vacation homes in the distance. A cool air, crisp and feeling of coming rain, was settling in around the lake.

And yet, Edan was burning up inside.

Seven

————◆————

What is the matter with me?

Yes, she was impetuous, but this was ridiculous.

Jenny fell onto her bed, covered her face and a groan with a pillow. Why why *why* had she kissed him like that? No warning, no build up—she'd gone right for the jugular. Sometimes, she amazed even herself with the things she did. Her face felt hot, and she wondered if he'd seen how embarrassed she was for having accosted him.

And yet, she wasn't exactly *sorry*, because that had been one super hot kiss. And lest there be any doubt, that aloof and distant man had participated *fully.*

Jenny fell asleep thinking of that kiss and woke up with the sensation of it still buzzing through her. She was debating whether or not she should apologize again when her phone rang. Jenny dug it out from beneath the bedspread and answered it.

"*Hey!*" Brooke shouted into the phone.

Jenny winced at her loud voice, then yawned. "Hi, Brooke."

"So I heard your boyfriend flaked on you," Brooke announced.

"Wait, what? How do you know that?" Jenny asked, then remembered. "Oh. Right. Bethany."

"She's worried about you. She said you won't answer your phone now."

"I won't?" Jenny yawned. "I was out last night and didn't have it on me."

"Keep it on you at all times. Is it true you're staying at some inn that's closed? Is that even safe?"

"Okay, I did not say that to Bethany," Jenny said, sitting up.

"She looked up quaint inns at Lake Haven online. How long are they going to let you stay there?"

"I have no idea," Jenny said. She thought of Edan. "Brooke—you won't believe what I did."

"Yes I will. Tell me."

"I kissed a man."

Brooke said nothing.

"I mean *I* kissed *him*. When he was holding a dirty sponge and couldn't fight me off."

There was a moment of silence, and then Brooke howled with laughter. "What do you mean, he couldn't fight you off because he was holding a sponge!"

"He was being polite. And then he told me to go home."

"Really!" Brooke said, sounding surprised.

Jenny told Brooke the whole story. Of arriving to

find the inn closed, of seeing Edan in a kilt. She told Brooke of the drive into East Beach and then the fish dinner, and how when she was leaving, she really meant to leave— "And then *boom,* I just kissed him."

"He didn't like it?"

"Yes. Not really. Maybe," Jenny said uncertainly. "Let's just say he didn't see it coming. But I like him, Brooke. I like him a lot."

There was a long pause, and then, "Jenny?" said in the careful tone one might use when addressing someone about to jump off a bridge. "You *just* broke up with Devin. Don't you think you ought to take a minute? Maybe do some introspection?"

"*Yes,* Brooke, of course I think I should take a minute. But sometimes you just get a sense about someone, and I have a sense about him. There's something that tells me he is kind of hurting and kind of alone, and he's so fucking *handsome,* and I don't know, I just *like* him. If you think about it, it's entirely possible that fate brought me here." She didn't add that she liked his quiet patience with her, which she knew was not easy. Or that he actually seemed to listen to her. Sometimes, anyway.

"And it's entirely possible you're reading far too much into it because you've been starved for good sex."

"Truth," Jenny admitted. Devin was *awful.* "And I'm not just saying that, Brooke. You and Vanessa and Bethany are always right about me. I'm impulsive, I need a job. I know I have to go home eventually. But I feel..." She paused. It was difficult for her to put into words, but she felt so at peace here. Like she was supposed to be at this inn. Her soul was sheltering here.

She also sensed that there was so much more lurking beneath the surface of Edan's amazing green eyes.

"Uh-oh," Brooke said. "You're not thinking—"

"No, no," Jenny said quickly. "I'm definitely not staying here. Even I know how insane that would be. Maybe a week, that's all. Which says I should leave well enough alone with him, right? Why start something I can't finish?"

"Who is talking right now?" Brooke asked. "This doesn't sound like Jenny, the queen of embrace your feelings and happiness. The guru of get in touch with your inner self. The yogi of love and peace—"

"Okay, all right, I get it," Jenny said.

"Look, no one is going to argue that you really need to get your shit together," Brooke said in a way that made Jenny suspect that she and Vanessa and Bethany had discussed it. "But you're there. So do whatever it takes. Explore it if you need to. But do *something,* Jen. What did your dad say, anyway?"

"I haven't actually talked to him," Jenny admitted. "I emailed him to tell him where I was and explain that Devin and I had broken up. He wrote back and told me not to spend all his money, then added a bunch of emojis that made no sense."

"That's it?"

"That's it."

Brooke clucked her tongue. "So maybe do what dear old Dad says—don't spend all his money and take care. But promise me that you'll get your head on straight?"

Jenny didn't think her head was on crooked to begin with. "Sure," she said.

"I'll call you in a few days. Oh, by the way, be

forewarned. Vanessa thinks she's lined up a possible job for you."

"*What?*"

"It's not much, but she knows someone in Santa Monica, and they're opening a coffee shop on the Promenade and looking for staff."

A coffee shop? Not exactly the career path Jenny was seeking. She could hear Vanessa in her head. *Just to get your feet wet. You have to get your feet wet.* "Great," she said. "Thanks for the warning."

When she and Brooke ended the call, she stared at the wall for a few moments. Vanessa was a beast of competency. If she found Jenny a job it was probably a decent one. She ought to take it and be grateful for it. Maybe she would. And then again...

She sat up and looked out the window. It was overcast. Maybe she'd take a hike into the hills and think about it. At least think about something other than how well Edan kissed.

When she was dressed, she made her way to the dining room. The door to the kitchen was open, and she could hear the banging of pots and pans. "Hello?"

A woman in thick-soled shoes with unnaturally bright hair piled atop her head emerged, carrying a tray full of salt and pepper sets. Jenny liked the look of her—she had a tattoo curling up her wrist. She stopped when she saw Jenny, clearly surprised. "Good morning," she said.

"Hi," Jenny returned.

The woman's gaze traveled down Jenny's body, taking in her tank top and jacket, her cargo shorts and her boots, the two long tails of hair that hung down her chest. She put down her tray of salt and pepper sets. "May I help you, then?"

"Is the restaurant open?"

"Well—" She wiped her hands on her apron and glanced over her shoulder. "I guess it could be, aye."

"I'm a guest," Jenny said. "And I'd love some breakfast."

"You're a guest... *here*?"

"Room 215. Is it okay if I sit down?"

"Aye, yeah, of course," the woman said. "I didna think we had any guests until the weekend." She took a step back, retrieving a menu from a stand and placed that in front of Jenny. "Coffee?"

"Please."

The woman pivoted about and went back into the kitchen. Jenny could hear her speaking loudly to someone else. That was followed by more banging of dishes and pots and doors. She reappeared a few minutes later with the coffee and an order pad. Jenny ordered eggs and ham, and the woman disappeared once more into the kitchen.

Jenny had drunk half her coffee when the woman returned with a plate of eggs, ham, and a caddy of dry toast. She set it all down on the table, wiped her hands on the towel she'd used to carry it out and said, "Plate is hot, mind."

"Thank you." Jenny picked up her fork and took a bite of eggs. She glanced up; the woman hadn't left.

"Do you mind if I ask—did you just check in?" the woman asked. "The inn's closing and we've only a pair of bookings left. I didna see one for today."

"I arrived Sunday night," Jenny said. "Long story, but I didn't know the inn was closed, and I showed up too late to go anywhere else. So Edan let me stay."

The woman blinked. "Edan?"

"Mr. Mackenzie."

"Oh aye, I know who he is. I'm Rosalyn, by the way."

"Oh!" Jenny said through a mouth full of egg. "You're the wedding! I'm Jenny."

"He told you about my wedding?"

"Sort of. I noticed he was wearing a kilt. I'd heard that in Scotland, men only wore kilts to formal occasions. So while he was making me a sandwich, I asked."

"He made you a *sandwich*!" It was not a question; it was a statement of utter disbelief.

It seemed like everyone around Lake Haven thought Edan incapable of making a sandwich. "Right in there, in the kitchen," Jenny said, pointing.

Rosalyn gaped at Jenny, her expressive brown eyes practically spinning with her thoughts. "I've never seen Edan make a sandwich for anyone. No' even himself. But I'm happy to hear he made it home in one piece. I worried—he'd had a wee bit to drink, aye? Freddie Montoya brung him home."

"Really?" Jenny said, thinking back to that night. "He seemed perfectly fine to me. He didn't really say much."

"*Ach,* well, he never says much," Rosalyn said. "Good on him, then," she said with an adamant nod of her head. "I worry about my old chum. No' that there's anything wrong with him, mind you, but he seems to be a wee bit too much in his own head, if you know what I mean."

"I do," Jenny agreed. "I noticed it last night at dinner."

Rosalyn stepped closer. "Beg your pardon—last night?"

"Yeah, we had dinner in the back. He was slightly more talkative than the night he made me a sandwich." She paused, thinking back to the way he'd looked at her, curious and confused and wary all at once. "A little more, anyway."

Rosalyn's eyes rounded like two pennies. "You must be joking. He invited you to dinner in the private quarters?"

"Oh, not like that," Jenny said with a laugh. "It was more like I invited myself and he took pity on me. The restaurant was closed, so I went around back to see if he had a bowl I could use. And there he was, grilling fish he'd caught." She smiled. "Fish was delicious."

Rosalyn stared off a moment. Then she looked at her watch. "Oh, bother, I've got to get on with it." She glanced up at Jenny. "Donna mind me being so nosy. I've known Edan for an age and like to keep an eye on him. Do you mean to go for a walk, then? It looks like rain. There are some extra brollies in the reception area."

Jenny was going to guess that a brolly was an umbrella, but she smiled and thanked her all the same, and Rosalyn went back into the kitchen.

She didn't need an umbrella. She'd checked her weather app—the rain wouldn't arrive until late this afternoon.

That would give her plenty of time to think things through.

Eight

It didn't rain. It *poured.*

Jenny and the two dogs had walked a little over two miles deep into the hills behind the Cassian Inn when the skies opened up and hosed her.

She should have grabbed a *brolly.*

She pulled the hood from her jacket up over her head and turned around to start back, assuming the terriers would be joining her. But the dogs had deserted her—she could see the dots of them running down the hill toward a red brick building.

Jenny trudged along behind them, picking her way down what was now a very muddy path. By the time she reached the red brick building she was thoroughly soaked. There was a parking lot and a sign that said, *Lake Haven Senior Home.*

She hurried inside to a vestibule entrance and

tried to shake the water off of her. It was useless. She draped her jacket over the umbrella bin and squeezed water from her hair as she dripped onto the welcome mat. Through a frosted glass door she could see shadowy forms of people moving around. One was moving closer.

A rush of cool air startled her when an elderly woman with kind eyes had opened the glass door. "Did you swim across the lake?" she asked jovially.

"Feels like it," Jenny said.

"Come in, dry off. Have some tea," the woman said.

"Thanks, but I'll just wait here for the rain to pass, if you don't mind. I have to find the two little dogs that were with me. They ran down here and I'm sure they are hiding around here somewhere."

"You must mean Mr. Mackenzie's dogs," she said. "He's put them in his car while he visits."

Jenny blinked. "Edan Mackenzie is *here*?"

"He is! He won't be long, I suspect. Poor man—Mr. Finlay doesn't know who he is any longer."

Who was Mr. Finlay? Jenny looked past the woman into the room behind her. There were several old people sitting about, some in wheelchairs, some at a table. A pair of caretakers in scrubs. And there, seated next to the window beside an old man was Edan. A very pretty and shapely caretaker was standing beside him, smiling with big doe eyes as she talked.

"Come in," the woman urged Jenny.

Jenny hesitantly stepped across the threshold, her eyes warily on Edan. It was still hard to believe that she'd boldly kissed him last night. She'd kissed him the way the young female caretaker probably wanted to kiss him this very minute. Oh yeah, Jenny could see it written all over her: The lean-in. The soft smile. The rapt attention to the few words he might utter.

Edan happened to glance in her direction. His gaze locked on hers and narrowed unhappily. He said something to the elderly man and stood up, put his hand on the man's shoulder, and then started toward Jenny.

She looked around for a place to hide.

"What are you doing here?" he demanded when he reached her.

"Drying off," she said, gesturing to herself. "I got caught in the rain. Turns out, my weather app is useless. It said it wouldn't start raining until this afternoon, so naturally the skies would—"

"I'll take you back to the inn, aye?" He put his hand on her elbow.

Jenny batted it away. "That's okay, I can walk back when it stops raining. I don't want to interrupt you."

Edan took her by the elbow again and wheeled her around to face the door. "How is that you keep appearing everywhere that I am?" he muttered.

"It's not hard—you pretty much exist in a two mile radius, have you noticed?"

"Let's go," he said low.

"Wait," Jenny protested. "You're not going to just go without saying goodbye, are you?"

"I said my goodbyes."

"Not to the gentleman, to the girl. She looks really sad, Edan—you should go back and say something to her. It's none of my business, but maybe ask her for a drink, because she is totally into you. She's practically drooling—"

"*Wheesht*," he muttered.

"Excuse me? That sounded like a sneeze. Is it a word? Never mind. Look at her," Jenny said, peering over her shoulder as he hustled her toward the entrance. "She looks as forlorn as the last puppy in the litter. At least thank her for taking care of your uncle."

He pushed the glass door open and said, "He is no' my uncle." He dropped his hand from the door, turned about and called across the room to the elderly woman, "Thank you, Mrs. Simmons. I'll come again next week."

"We'll all look forward to it!" Mrs. Simmons said.

Apparently satisfied, Edan tried to move Jenny out the door, then, but she resisted. "Say goodbye to the girl."

"What is the *matter* with you?" he demanded.

"I've been that girl. I'm not suggesting you marry her, I'm suggesting you say goodbye."

She could see Edan gritting his teeth. But he slowly turned and said, "Thank you, Phoebe."

"Of course!" Phoebe said with a thousand-watt brightness. "If there's anything I can do for you, anything at all, just call me. You have my number, right?"

"Aye," he said, and practically pushed Jenny through the glass doors before him.

She scarcely had time to grab her jacket before he was steering her out the door and to his car.

"I'm wet!" she cried when he opened the passenger door.

"Get in, get in," he said.

She slipped into the passenger seat, and the two dogs instantly surged forward, their feet on the console between the seats, their tongues working in tandem on Jenny's ear until she pushed them off. They left behind smeared paw prints on the leather. "Oh my God, I'm so sorry," she said, and wiped the console with the sleeve of her jacket.

"Never mind it," Edan said as he started the car.

"Why are you being so weird? Is it Phoebe?"

"No," he said, and looked the other way.

"Who were you visiting?"

"Mr. Finlay."

When Edan did not add any helpful details, Jenny said, "Not your uncle."

"Mr. Finlay was the maintenance man at the inn for many years. He has no one. No family."

It was awfully kind of Edan to visit him. Jenny knew how people drifted away when someone was ill. Her father had lost all his friends as the junk around him had piled up.

And then, out of nowhere, comes a girlfriend. *Jesus.*

"Who's going to look in on him when you go back to Scotland?" she asked curiously.

His jaw tightened and he gave her a pointed look that could be interpreted to mean she should stop talking before he got really mad.

"Because you're going back soon, right?" she asked, hoping that he'd had some miraculous change of heart overnight and would say no.

"When did you say you were checking out?"

"Still thinking about it." She didn't have a good answer for him. Because she was looking at his mouth, remembering last night and feeling tiny electric pulses zinging through her. "So listen, Edan, about last night—"

"No need," he said quickly.

"I should not have done that."

"You've already apologized. Donna say more."

"Okay," she agreed. "But the thing is, while I *am* sorry for kissing you, I kind of liked it. Actually, I liked it a lot. You should know you're a good kisser."

Edan groaned softly and glanced out the window.

"I'm not even sure why I'm telling you this," she said with a small laugh of mortification. "But sometimes, it seems like the things that need to be said are not said, and the things that shouldn't be said are. All that to say, I feel like you should know that I had a great time last night."

"I am confused," he said. "Did you no' just suggest I take a woman out for a drink?"

"I can see where that might be confusing," she agreed. "I didn't suggest it because I actually wanted you to, but because I felt sorry for her. She obviously has it bad for you. And when I noticed it, I thought, maybe I should say what's been on *my* mind. It's kind of a weird compulsion I have."

"I've noticed," he said. They had reached the inn, and Edan pulled into the little courtyard. He put the car in park and turned his head to her. He awkwardly put his hand on her knee. "Jenny. Lass. I enjoyed our dinner, too, aye? But I must be verra clear—I'll no' encourage Phoebe or anyone else, because I am leaving at the end of the month to repair a relationship with my fiancée, aye? I love her."

He didn't have to say *that*.

"There is no possibility of anything between us," he added, and removed his hand.

Jenny hadn't said there was and she tried not to be offended by the words *no possibility*. "Okay," she said breezily. "But did *you* like the kiss?"

He stared at her for a long moment. "Did you hear what I said, then?"

"Loud and clear. Did you like it?"

His eyes dipped to her mouth and lingered. And then he opened the door.

As he got out of the car and let the dogs out, Jenny shouted at him, "I think this clearly indicates that you did!"

Edan shut the door and dashed to the entry with the dogs close behind.

Jenny sighed. She never did these things right. She got out, too, and ran to the entry. She paused just inside to gather her wits and remove her jacket when she heard Edan say, "It's good to have you back. I'm glad to see you before I go, aye?"

Jenny jerked around to see three well-heeled gentlemen standing beside a mountain of luggage. They'd also turned around to have a look at her, just as Jenny realized her wet tank revealed more of her than she liked—her nipples were jutting through the fabric. All the male eyes in this room were on them.

The darkly handsome man standing in the middle of the threesome smirked and muttered in Italian, "*Lei un mendicante?*"

Jenny gasped. "I most certainly am not a beggar! I was very obviously caught in the rain! Have you looked outside? It's *pouring.*"

The three men exchanged a startled look. Edan arched a surprised brow, too, peering closely at her.

"*Parli Italiano?*" the man asked.

"Of course I speak Italian," Jenny groused. "Doesn't everyone?"

"No," Edan said, inexplicably cheerful as he

moved behind the reception desk.

The gentleman who had called her a beggar stepped forward—cautiously, she noted—and extended his hand. He spoke again in Italian, "I am Lorenzo. Lorenzo Bartolotti. Who might I have the *very great* pleasure of meeting?"

It was no pleasure, it was embarrassing. And it didn't help to see Edan actually smiling behind the three of them, clearly enjoying her discomfort. "Jenny Turner." She ignored his hand and folded her arms tightly across her body instead. "I'm going to my room now." She gave them all a withering look before marching off down the hall with the clothes clinging to her and her boots squeaking loudly and her thoughts racing around Edan and the fact she didn't have this perfect little inn to herself any longer.

Nine

———◆———

After a bath and a nap, Jenny felt much better about her disastrous morning. The sun had peeked out, too, which helped her get over her unreliable weather app.

She'd also found a little clarity, too. This morning, her head had been filled with that sexy as hell kiss. But now, having seen the young woman at the care home look so longingly at Edan, and recalling his sober expression when he'd announced he loved his ex, Jenny had come to a few conclusions.

One: She loved it here, but she couldn't stay indefinitely without purpose.

Two: Edan was going back to find his love and that was that.

Three: She could back to California and face her new family dynamic instead of avoiding it, and maybe take the job Vanessa had found for her.

Four: Or she could buy this inn.

The thought had come to her as she'd soaked in the tub. Edan was leaving, the inn was going on the market. Why not her? She had the money. Well, okay, her dad did, but he would be happy to loan it to her. This was exactly what he'd told her to do the night he'd invited her to dinner at Lolo's Lounge and had sprung Cathy on her.

At the time, Jenny had thought the invitation was odd because her father rarely got out—between his work and his inability to find anything in his house, he pretty much kept to himself. Or so she'd thought. The moment she'd walked into the restaurant, her gut had sank, because he was sitting there next to a woman with a short crop of unnaturally yellow hair. Both of them were smiling at her. Too sunnily. Too eagerly.

"Jen, sweetie, I'd like you to meet Cathy," her father had said, and his chest had puffed up a little, and his eyes had taken on a sheen of delight.

Jenny could hardly speak she'd been so shocked. "But how?" she'd asked. "How could you not tell me, Dad?"

"I was afraid you might, you know, insert yourself," he'd said jovially.

They were going to live together, he said. Cathy was going to help him clean out his house.

Great, she'd thought. *Good luck with that.* "I've tried to help you clean out the house for years," she'd reminded him. Years she'd never had anyone sleep over. Years of friendships she'd never had because she was afraid someone would find out their dirty secret. It wasn't until she went away to college and attached herself to Vanessa, Brooke and Bethany that she had actual friends, and the only reason she did was because they were on the other side of the country from her family's dysfunction.

But her father had smiled sympathetically and said, "It's not your job to fix your dad, sweetie. It's your job to live *your* life. You know what I wish? I wish you would find that thing that makes you happy. I wish you would find the place where you fit." He'd reached across the table and had taken her hand in his. "Cathy and I both hope you will at last feel free to go and live your life."

Jenny didn't know what was more jarring—that her father was essentially telling her to get out of his life? Or that he had discussed it with Cathy?

But on the other hand, had it not been for him and Cathy, she never would have gone with Devin to escape. She never would have found the Cassian Inn. And she *loved* it here. She loved the lake, she loved the old Victorian mansion, she loved being far away from her awful childhood home.

This was where she belonged. It was becoming clearer and clearer to her.

So she grabbed her laptop, and headed for the lounge so she could email her dad about it.

As she walked down the hallway, she happened to see one of the Italian men walk into the lounge ahead of her.

She detoured.

She went outside into the sun and followed a path that took her past the inn and into the woods, and up to the top of a small hill that overlooked the lake. To her delight, she discovered a bench. Jenny put aside her laptop and sat down. Here was the opportunity to meditate she'd hoped for this morning, and she tucked her feet up beneath her, pressed her palms together at her heart center, and bowed her head.

The goal of her meditation was to clear her mind and breathe before she emailed her father, But her mind was not clear—she kept seeing Edan Mackenzie and the way he looked at her, even when telling her there was *no possibility.* Unfortunately, she was thinking of him so intently that she could practically hear him.

Wait a minute—she *could* hear him. And he was talking. In complete sentences. Jenny opened her eyes and looked wildly about. She could definitely *hear* him, but she couldn't see him. She stood up, following the sound of his voice to the tree line. She peered into the woods and realized that the cluster of trees to the north side of the bench was nothing more than a copse. On the other side of that copse was a cemetery. She could see the top of Edan's dark head—he was squatting beside a headstone and he was *talking.* Holy cow, the man was talking to a ghost.

Jenny suddenly realized she was watching him in a private, unguarded moment, which mortified her, particularly since he already believed she was stalking him. She hurried back to the bench, grabbed her laptop, and fled down the path. In her haste to get as far from his as she could, she took the wrong fork in the path and emerged in back of the inn.

"Close call," she muttered, and tucking her laptop up under her arm, began the walk around the inn to the entrance courtyard.

"*Ciao,* Jenny Turner."

Startled, Jenny almost dropped her computer. She hadn't seen one of the Italians sitting on the wooden bench next to the hedgerow. He smiled, his teeth brilliantly white in the sunlight, and came to his feet.

"You are dry and you are smiling. *Bella, bella.* Now, this day is made beautiful for both of us," he said with a charming smile.

"It's still a little muddy," she pointed out.

"There is not so much of the mud. Come, sit," he said, and gestured to the bench.

She eyed him skeptically.

"I am Lorenzo," he said. "We've met."

"Very briefly."

"*Si,* but I will not bite," he said breezily. "Not unless you ask me to." He winked and patted the seat next to him.

He seemed fairly harmless as far as Italian males went. Plus, he'd just called her *bella*, and Jenny was not immune to the power of a compliment. So she sat, but kept a good distance between them.

"So?" he said, opening his arms. "You are an American who speaks Italian," he said in Italian.

"Obviously. And you're an Italian who speaks English," she said in English.

"Obviously," he said, and grinned at her. "But many Italians speak English. It is the language of the world, no? Not so many Americans speak Italian."

"I don't really speak it. I remember it."

Her summers in Italy had ended with her mother's death. Her grandmother had died the following year. "*Broken heart,*" her father had said.

"My grandmother was Italian, and I spent summers with her in Liguria."

"Ah, charming Liguria!" He kissed the tips of his fingers. "*Bello.* And now, you are at charming Lake Haven. Do you have a grandmother here, as well?" he asked slyly.

"Actually, I am here on something of a personal

journey."

He looked at her blankly.

"Umm…let me think. *Spirituale viaggio.*"

"Ah, of course, a journey of spirits!" he proclaimed.

"Something like that," Jenny agreed, deciding it wasn't worth the effort to clarify. "This is the perfect place for it, you know? So beautiful and pure here. It's like one step closer to heaven."

"No, this is no good, to be closer to heaven," he said, wagging a finger at her. "If you reach heaven, then what have you left?"

"Who knows? That's the beauty of discovery! You never know what's around the corner. And you, Signore Bartolotti? What brings you here?"

"You wound me with this *signore*," he said. "I am for you, Lorenzo."

"Okay. Lorenzo," she said smiling.

"And this?" he said, gesturing grandly to the inn and the grounds. "This is like home to me," he said, patting his palm against his heart. "I come to Lake Haven many times."

"Why?"

"Why!" he scoffed. "Look around you, Jenny Turner. As you say, *bellisimo.* And I fish."

What was it about fishing that was so appealing? She didn't get it.

"But this time?" He waved his hand, and the two gold and diamond rings on his fingers caught the sunlight and almost blinded her. "This time, I do not fish."

"Why not?"

"Because, my *bellissima Americana*," he said, his eyes welling, "I cannot."

"Is something wrong?" Jenny asked as he dabbed at his eyes. "Are you all right?"

"*Si, si*," he said, dragging a finger beneath one eye. But then, just as quickly he said, "*No!* How can I be all right when my heart has broken?" He suddenly surged forward and buried his face in his hands.

"Oh," Jenny said, wincing a little. "Can I help?"

"No. Everything is wrong," he moaned. "Elizabetta, she is through with me." He sat up and rubbed his eyes. "She's thrown me aside like garbage," he said. "I've made mistakes, many mistakes, I admit it freely. Yet I love her, and I am paralyzed by the thought of losing her." He suddenly twisted about, and grabbed Jenny's hand. "Have you ever lost someone you cared for very deeply?"

"*Si*," Jenny said, nodding. "Not a lover, but you know, Grandma—"

"There is nothing more painful than this loss," he said, tapping his chest with his fist. "It eats at me every day like *cancer*. That is why I've come here, Jenny Turner—"

"Actually, you can just call me Jenny—"

"Because I cannot bear to see Elizabetta and know that she hates me. I've come here, to the place I know so well, to put her out of my mind," he said, shaking his fist at his head. "And yet, I can't stop thinking of her. I can't stop loving her because she demands it."

He suddenly slumped against the back of the bench. "It's hopeless. I'm ruined. I will never recover. I will never love again."

Not likely. "So…" Jenny said, enjoying his performance. "May I ask what happened?"

"Oh," he said, flicking his wrist. "Nothing to

cause such heartache." He shifted his gaze away from her.

"Well, something must have happened," she prodded. A movement caught her eye, and she looked up—Edan had appeared on the drive with a bucket in hand. He slowed his step when he saw the two of them there.

Lorenzo didn't notice Edan at all. He was too busy holding court. "I love her too much, what more can I say?"

"You can say what you did," Jenny suggested, and waved at Edan. She got a lift of his chin in return. At least he didn't hightail it into the entry hall and lock the door.

Lorenzo sniffed. He picked a piece of imaginary lint from his trousers. "It was not so big," he said. "I kissed another woman in the heat of the moment. That is all."

"*Wow,*" Jenny said, momentarily distracted from Edan.

"It was not my fault!" he insisted. "She kissed *me,* and yet no one will believe it."

"Oh, I believe it," Jenny muttered as she watched Edan walk on and disappear around the corner. "But it's not like she attacked you and pinned you down when you were holding a sponge and forced herself on you... was it?"

Lorenzo sighed. "You women, you are all alike," he said gruffly. "So easily offended, no? Very well, I made a mistake. But I *die* with this mistake. I would do anything to have my Elizabetta back. *In qualche modo!* I would gouge out my eyes—"

"That's a little much," Jenny said.

"I would not joke about such a thing. What else

can I do?"

"Well, I'm no expert," Jenny said, settling back, preparing to be an expert. "But I would start with a *heartfelt* apology. You probably said something like, 'I'm sorry.'"

"Yes, of course, this is what I said," he insisted, his hand stabbing the air with each word. "I am sorry, Elizabetta. But her friends, they talk in her ear," he said, making a gesture of chattering. "They turn her against me."

"Mmm," Jenny said.

"Mmm? What does this mean, *mmm*?"

"It means that wasn't enough. You said you were sorry, and she told her friends, and they were all like, girl, you've got to be kidding. I think you should send her an insanely expensive bouquet of flowers if you haven't already. Maybe you could write her a letter explaining what she means to you. Not a text—an actual letter. And you should tell her why you made such a totally boneheaded mistake."

Lorenzo glanced curiously at her.

"*Stupido* mistake," she clarified for him. "You need to grovel."

"Ah." He tilted his head to one side, considering what she'd said. "Do you think this can work?"

"I have no idea," Jenny admitted. "I obviously don't know your girlfriend. But I know a little about women and I know it can't hurt."

"*Si, si,*" he said, nodding emphatically. "I will do this today, and you will help me," he said.

"What? *No*! That is *not* what I meant—"

"*Grazie, grazie,* Jenny Turner," he said, and suddenly took her by the shoulders and yanked her forward, giving her a kiss on one cheek, and then the other. "Come, we write the letter now," Lorenzo said, and stood up, taking her hand. "Look, you see? You've come with a computer."

Jenny tried to protest, but Lorenzo was determined.

She did not notice that Edan had come back around to the courtyard. He was standing at the edge of it, watching Lorenzo usher her inside to write his letter.

Ten

Edan didn't know how things like this happened. The last few days had seemed almost as if he'd imagined them, they were so foreign to his way of living. He didn't know how fully formed women suddenly threw their arms around men they scarcely knew and kissed them. He didn't know how that same impulsive woman was suddenly inseparable with another man she'd only just met.

But that is precisely what had happened with Jenny and Lorenzo.

One moment, she was stomping through his reception area with clothes clinging to her enticingly curvy body, and the next, she and Lorenzo Bartolotti had their heads together, bent over a computer, murmuring in Italian.

They'd even dined together last night. Jenny had

tried to include him in their party, but Edan was not going to suffer being the third wheel at that table, particularly after Lorenzo's brothers had left the Cassian Inn, bound for a proper resort with a proper golf course. And a proper bar. And proper dancing girls.

And again the next morning, there went Lorenzo and Jenny toddling off to East Beach on some mission of importance, chattering away as if they'd known each other all their lives.

Edan should have been relieved that the loquacious lass had something to occupy her. He should have been grateful that Lorenzo had come along and removed the unexpected problem of her in his head and in his life. God knew he had enough to do without her nattering on in his ear.

But he was not relieved. He was, surprisingly, miffed. And it didn't help that his dogs were moping about as if she'd left them behind. How long did she intend to stay and wreak havoc, anyway?

"I donna understand it," he said to Clara's headstone. "It's no' as if I care, aye?" He glanced sidelong at the headstone for a moment, feeling as if Clara was giving him the side eye from some celestial perch. All right, perhaps it was true that Jenny had uncovered some feeling in him. It was lying there, visible where his grief over Audra was beginning to rot through.

Jenny had set him on fire, and for a man who had not been set afire in a while, that was a dangerous thing to have done. Now he wondered if she was the sort of bird who flirted and carried on with any fucking penis that crossed her path. That thought was followed by the equally exasperating thought that it wasn't his business. All those thoughts together put him in a very foul mood the following afternoon, which was much remarked upon by Rosalyn. She said his demeanor was colder than Highland snow. That his scowl could curdle milk. And then she'd made the mistake of summoning him to the kitchen to tell him she needed flour.

"If you need flour, Ros, you'd best say so before five o'clock. It's no' as if the markets stay open for the Cassian Inn, is it?" he'd snapped. "Now I'll have to drive all the way to Black Springs."

Sandra, who had been helping Rosalyn in the kitchen, gasped. In all the years she'd known him, she likely had never heard Edan say something so coldly.

"I've got a sack of flour," she said. " I'll just fetch it." She fled the kitchen.

"What's put your knickers in a twist?" Rosalyn demanded. She was not as easily put off as Sandra.

Edan shook his head. He stood in the dining room, his gaze fixed on the windows that looked out over the garden and the drive. He was aware that Rosalyn's gaze was boring into him. "I've no' seen you like this since Audra left. Are you ill, then?"

"I'm no' ill." But he might be at any moment, for he happened to notice the happy alliance of Italy and America rumbling toward the inn in Lorenzo's red car. Lorenzo always hired a red car, the bloody rooster.

"Well, you've been acting like an utter dobber for two days now."

Edan rolled his eyes. He would let that insult slide, particularly as he couldn't give a good reason he was in such a foul mood without revealing too much. He would keep his torment to himself, thank you. But that was precisely the thing—there shouldn't have *been* any torment. It was one bloody kiss! He was going back to Scotland, goddammit, and Audra would take him back. He'd spent the last two years of his life working on that relationship, and he'd spent the last six months planning the repair of it.

He steadfastly refused to let the little devil in him ask why he would go back to a woman who, if he was being honest, had never seemed overly happy with him, and had always found reason to complain. She was Scottish, that was why—she didn't belong in America any more than he did. And *he* was Scottish dammit, no matter that he held dual citizenship, courtesy of his American mother. Audra was from Balhaire, just like him. He was *not* an American.

He did not belong here.

Lorenzo's red car suddenly screeched into the courtyard to a halt. Lorenzo hopped out.

"Oh that bloke," Rosalyn said, startling Edan. He hadn't realized she was standing behind him. "Is *he* the reason you're acting strange?"

"I'm no' acting strange," Edan said, and turned away from the window before Jenny emerged from the car.

"Hmm," Rosalyn said, her eyes narrowing slightly. She folded her arms and stared out the window. "What's the American bird doing with him? What's the American bird doing *here*? Seems passing strange to me that she's at the inn with nothing to do here."

"How would I know?" Edan asked irritably.

Rosalyn shrugged. "Does it no' seem a wee bit odd to you that she stays on? We're no' known for attracting the fun crowd, are we? And we're closing!

Why is she here? What does she want?"

"Obviously, she's found a friend," he said, gesturing toward the window.

"Seems odd, that's all," Rosalyn said again, then looked at the clock on the wall. "I best get to work. The Pettimores like their supper at six. Perhaps you'd like to take an aspirin and lay down for a bit, aye?" She glanced pertly over her shoulder at Edan before disappearing into the kitchen.

Edan was more than happy to leave and walked out of the dining room. Rosalyn could see through him at times when he did not care to be transparent. Usually, he appreciated that someone was looking out for him, because God knew he'd managed to arrange his life so that no one else did. But today, he could do without her scrutiny.

He strolled into the reception area, said hello to Mr. and Mrs. Pettimore, and listened politely as Mrs. Pettimore excitedly reported seeing an indigo bunting during their bird-watching excursion today. Behind the elderly couple, Jenny and Lorenzo entered, talking and laughing, all jolly and bright like one of those Christmas advertisements that came on the telly. A picture postcard for youth and beauty and…well, Lorenzo was a picture of debauchery, generally, but a handsome picture of debauchery nonetheless.

That made Edan even more cross.

When the Pettimores had wandered off in search of brandy, Jenny hopped over to where Edan was standing. "There you are!" Her eyes were shining, her smile bloody bright.

"Aye."

"I wanted to ask you about this," she said, and dug into her woven bag. She pulled out a handful of brochures and searched through them until she found one. "This," she said, holding it up to him. He took the brochure from her hand. *Fishing Tours of the Cassian Hills and Lake Haven on ATVs! Drive old logging trails through ancient forests home to native wildlife species such as whitetail deer, red fox, and peregrine falcons. Visit pristine hidden lakes and cast your lure...*

He handed it back to her. "Aye?"

"We'd like to take the tour. It says right here that it begins at the Cassian Inn."

"It did. We no longer offer the tour."

"What? Lorenzo has taken it," she said.

"*Si*, we fished, Edan," Lorenzo said. "Do you remember?"

How could Edan possibly forget it? Lorenzo had come to the lake with a woman, and she'd worn high-heeled sandals and an extremely short skirt to fish. "That lake is remote," he said to Jenny. "And I thought you were generally against fishing."

"I am. I *was*. But I didn't know you could take an ATV to get there. I've always wanted to ride an ATV."

"Unfortunately, we've only two ATVs. The guide must have one."

"We'll ride together," Lorenzo offered, smiling. He put his hand on Jenny's shoulder.

Edan stared at that hand, irrationally angry with it.

"Is it possible for us to arrange it?" Jenny asked. "Lorenzo said the scenery is even more breathtaking than here at the inn."

"We can manage, can we not, Edan?" Lorenzo asked, as if they were old chums. No, they couldn't manage. Mr. Finlay, who generally conducted those tours, couldn't remember who he was, much less how to guide anyone up into the hills.

"Aye, we can manage," he heard himself say.

"Hooray!" Jenny said, clapping her hands. "What time should we be ready in the morning? I hope not too early. I would like to practice yoga before we go. I was going to practice this morning, but I heard all these voices and when I went outside, there were four men standing on the tee box. It was like *seriously* early," she said looking back and forth between Jenny and Lorenzo. "I never knew people who golfed were out as soon as the sun comes up."

"No, no, in Italy, these golfers, they come to hit the ball later in the day. No one begins very early in Italy," Lorenzo offered.

"I can vouch for that," Jenny said. "*Soprattutto in Liguria*," she said, and the two of them laughed.

"Nine," Edan said.

"Excuse me?" Jenny asked.

Her eyes were sparkling. She was happy with this bastard Lorenzo. She'd kissed Edan and now she was laughing it up with Lorenzo. Edan's pulse was beginning to pick up steam. "If you'd like to take the ATV tour, it begins at nine o'clock, aye?"

"Perfect!" she exclaimed. "Thanks, Edan. You're the best."

What the bloody hell did that mean? The best of the two men standing here? The best ATV arranger? The best innkeeper, the best kisser, the best at wanting to take her clothes off and thrust into her?

"Hey, you want to come to join us for dinner?" she asked. "I hear the special is shepherd's pie."

"No. Thank you."

"Maybe tomorrow."

"So you will still be here tomorrow," he coolly remarked.

"Well, I'm not going to miss the ATV excursion." She glanced back at Lorenzo. "Shall we check and see if you got a response to your email?"

"*Si, si,*" he said. He put his hand on the small of Jenny's back and half-saluted, half-waved at Edan as they went off to look at email.

Edan walked calmly back to his office. He shut the door behind him, then ran both hands over the crown of his head, then kicked his office chair so hard that it slammed into the filing cabinet and knocked off two fishing trophies.

What was the matter with him? Why did he feel so protective and desirous and so bloody *jealous*? She was not his responsibility. He wasn't even interested. He'd calmly explained this would not work. She could do whatever the hell she wanted.

Just not with Lorenzo Bartolotti.

Lorenzo was a ladies' man, a player, and Jenny...what did she know of men like that? Lorenzo had brought more than one woman to the Cassian Inn over the years.

No matter—Jenny wasn't his problem. He didn't have to mope about it like a sullen little boy. Nonetheless, Edan stalked around to his private quarters with Wilbur and Boz, fed them, and retreated to his study to sulk.

He'd managed to engross himself in a book when he heard commotion outside and got up to have a look. From a window in the tower, he saw Lorenzo help Jenny into his red car and then pour himself into the driver's side and speed away.

Edan went back to his book. But he no longer saw words. He saw sparkling blue eyes and lips that should be kissed.

And not by fucking Lorenzo Bartolotti.

At quarter until nine the next morning, Hugh helped Edan bring the ATVs around. "You're quite certain you donna want me to take them?" Hugh asked again.

"Thank you, but I'm quite sure," Edan said.

Hugh did not seem convinced. He looked at the ATVs. "I wouldna mind a bit of fishing. Looks like a fine day for it, too."

"I doubt the fish are biting," Edan muttered, and fastened the fishing poles on the back of one of the ATVs.

At ten to nine, Jenny walked out onto the drive. She'd tied up her hair into a loose knot at her crown, and she was wearing cutoff jean shorts that hugged her hips and left bare glorious legs that disappeared into some colorful rain boots. "Good morning!" she said cheerfully. "Are you here to see us off?"

"I'm you're guide."

She gasped with surprise. And then her face broke into a sunny smile. "That's *fantastic*! I'm so glad you can get out, Edan. And not because the woman in East Beach said so, but because the weather is wonderful, the scenery is wonderful, and since you're leaving, you really ought to take the time to enjoy it before you go. Plus, you were, like, super grumpy yesterday," she added, and playfully punched him in the arm.

"I've got a rather busy job," he reminded her.

"Job, schmob," she said. "Admit it—you *like* to ride ATVs. It's the boy in you. I know you want everyone to think you're a badass fisherman—"

"I never—"

"But an ATV is like a puppy," she said, talking over him. "Boys and men can't resist puppies or ATVs. If I'm not mistaken, there is some actual science behind that." She paused, tapped her lip with one finger. "No...no, I'm mistaken. I think what I actually read is that men and boys are more likely to be *killed* by ATVs. Which one's mine?" she asked, twisting around to the ATVs. "I like the blue one."

"They are exactly the same."

"Well, not exactly, smart guy. One is blue and one is green. Are there helmets? I think we ought to have—"

He held out a helmet.

"Look at *you*," she said, smiling coyly. "You've thought of everything. But *I* thought about sandwiches. Rosalyn was nice enough to make some." She held up the bag she carried. "She made liverwurst for the guide," she said wrinkling her nose. "She said to be sure and tell the guide it was especially for him. Will you hold this a moment?" she asked, shoving the bag at him.

Edan grabbed it just before she dropped it. She put the helmet on her head, her hands on her hips, and dipped into a model's pose. "How do I look?"

Beautiful. "Ridiculous," he said, and handed her the bag, then stepped forward to tighten the strap of her helmet. Jenny lifted her chin and smiled up at him, her gaze first locked on his eyes, then sliding down, to his mouth as he fumbled with the straps of her helmet.

His blood began to stir. "Donna smile so," he

grumbled. "It's distracting."

"Is it? Sorry, but smiling and yoga are my thing. You should try them sometime. You'd be amazed at how much happier you'd feel about life if you did either one. Double the feels if you do them simultaneously."

He allowed himself to look in her eyes. "I couldna possibly smile at so many things as you. You'd smile at a rock, I think." He cinched up the strap beneath her chin.

"Better to smile at a rock than to kick it." She winked. And then blithely faded away from him and walked over to have a look at the ATV.

At nine o'clock, Jenny was staring at the door of the reception. Edan took a seat on the bench, happy to watch her bottom in the shorts as she wandered about. "I wonder where Lorenzo is?" she said idly, and sat down on the bench so close to Edan that her knee touched his.

Edan thought about moving his leg away. He didn't. "Lorenzo is on Italian time," he said. He stretched his arms out across the back of the bench. If Lorenzo never showed up, he wouldn't mind.

Jenny leaned back and rested her neck against his arm. It was such a familiar thing to do, something a child or a spouse would do, and oddly, it made Edan feel lonesome. Audra had never been so easy with him. Bloody hell, was he going to be maudlin now, too?

He was beginning to wonder if he even knew himself anymore. He'd been perfectly fine before this girl had come in and banged away at his reception bell. He'd known exactly what he wanted and needed to do. But then she'd come and now he was questioning everything.

He looked away.

"I've had a wonderful few days here," Jenny suddenly announced. "Do you ever wonder how you ended up in one place instead of another? Like...I ended up at Mount Holyoke because my dad knew someone who knew the dean and told me about it. Otherwise, I never would have heard of Mount Holyoke. If I hadn't gone to school there, I never would have met my best friends. And then I ended up as an art teacher because I got involved with an anti-bullying group—"

"You were bullied?"

"Oh no. I was trying to help someone who had been bullied. Turns out, he was the bully, but *anyway,* I met this man in the group whose mother was on the board of a private school. What if I hadn't tried to help that kid? I never would have been an art teacher."

He was certain there was more to the story, because so far, it was illogical.

"It's just strange how things have a way of working out." She turned her head to look at him. "And then I started thinking about why I ended up here, and I think maybe because I needed to help someone."

He felt a funny little curl in the pit of his stomach. Did he need help? Did he need someone to pull him out of the muck of his life? No, he was fine. He was *fine.* "I donna need help," he said.

Color crept into Jenny's cheeks. "FYI, you've made that abundantly clear," she said. "But I wasn't talking about you. I was talking about Lorenzo." She looked away. "And I was talking about *me.*"

"Jenny Turner!" came the shout of a familiar

voice.

"There he is!" Jenny said brightly, and hopped up off the bench and away from Edan as Lorenzo came striding outside.

Eleven

The ATV tour was nothing as promised in the brochure Jenny had found at Lakeshore Coffee in East Beach, and she was fairly certain it was Edan's fault. They stopped twice; once at a very narrow valley filled with trees, and Jenny listened politely as Edan announced that the birds that lived there had gone north for the summer. Next, they stopped alongside a babbling brook and Edan said fox and deer probably drank here, but he couldn't know for certain. And then he promptly returned to his ATV and took off, leaving Jenny and Lorenzo scrambling to catch up.

When they reached the lake—which was more of a giant pond, really—Edan took the tackle and three poles from the cage on his ATV and walked down to the water's edge without a word.

"Don't you want your liverwurst?" Jenny shouted

after him, holding up the sandwich bag.

Edan said something in response over his shoulder, and it didn't sound very appreciative. Jenny sighed, fished a sandwich from the bag, and dropped the bag.

She should never have kissed that stupid, stubborn, ridiculous man. He'd gone entirely weird since she had.

"Jenny Turner, look, see what I have," Lorenzo said anxiously, holding out his phone. "Elizabetta had responded."

"Has she?" Jenny asked absently. She was still watching Edan walk down to the lake's edge. He had on knee-high rubber boots, faded jeans, and a fitted black tee. He looked rugged and sexy and competent, the kind of guide you'd hope to get on some Alaska excursion into the wild in case there were bears to be wrestled or elk to be caught. He was also so damn stoic she wanted to punch him right in the kisser.

Lorenzo followed her gaze out to Edan. "Don't worry for him, *bella.* He likes to be alone."

"No one likes to be alone *that* much."

"Ah, but Eddy, he's wanted alone since the woman, how do you say, dumped him." He made a slashing motion across his throat.

"You know about that?" she asked curiously.

He shrugged. "I was here."

Oh. *Oh.* "Do you know what happened?" she asked, perhaps a bit too eagerly.

"A man can never truly know the heart of a woman," he said with a dismissive flick of his wrist. "It is impossible."

"It's not *impossible*—"

"But this woman, she did not love him," he said.

Jenny gasped. "How do you know?"

"How do I know," he said gruffly. "I *know*." He glanced at his hands. "She told me. Eddy, he is quiet. He likes this life. She came here for him, but she didn't like it so much. She is a woman for dancing, and for life. He is a man for books and fishing."

Jenny glanced at Edan. She liked books. And quiet. Not so much the fishing.

"We went to a dance club once," Lorenzo said, squatting down beside Jenny.

"You took Edan's fiancée dancing?" she asked disapprovingly.

He arched his thick brows. "Why do you look at me like this? I did not touch her." He suddenly smiled. "But she *wanted* me to." He chuckled low and leaned closer. "She *begged* me to do it."

Jenny clucked her tongue and turned her attention to Edan again.

"It is very sad," Lorenzo said, "to love a woman who will not love you in return. But she was very beautiful, this girl. He thought he could make her happy, but this girl, she cannot be happy anywhere, I think."

"I love here," Jenny murmured.

"She lied to him from the beginning. He does not trust easily the women now."

Who could blame him? Jenny couldn't imagine how demoralizing that must have been. Mainly because she'd never really been in love. Not like that, anyway. She sank down onto a rock and unwrapped her sandwich. She had always been an emotional eater. "No wonder he's always so…quiet," she said.

"Eh," Lorenzo said. "This is good for him. This is how he…what is this word…griefs."

"Grieves," she muttered. "I feel so bad for him."

"*Anh,*" Lorenzo said with a shrug. "The man was dumped. These things happen."

"I know. But I don't like them to happen to people I…" For once, Jenny actually thought about what she was about to say, and decided against admitting she had feelings for him.

"Aha," Lorenzo said, nodding sagely. "You *like* him, our Eddy."

"No I don't," she scoffed.

"*Ach,* don't deny this. It has distorted your face."

So much for not saying anything—apparently her distorted face did her talking. "Of *course* I like him. He's a nice man, and he seems lonely." She tried to appear nonchalant about it by biting into her sandwich. But judging by the way Lorenzo's hands went to his hips, she'd failed.

"Why did you not tell me this?" he demanded.

Jenny looked at him like he'd lost his mind. "I hardly know you, Lorenzo. I'm not going to admit everything in my head just because you did."

"*Vaffanculo,* we are friends! Is it not my friend who has helped me make things better with Elizabetta? Here, see what she says," he said, waving his phone at her.

Jenny groaned. She took the phone from him, squinting at the cramped writing. Speaking Italian was quite a lot easier than reading it. She didn't understand all what Elizabetta had typed in her shorthand Italian, but she gathered that Elizabetta had seen some promise in Lorenzo's apology. And she wrote that she would like to speak to Lorenzo in person with the hope of patching things together.

Jenny was about 75 percent sure that's what the

email said. "Well this is fantastic," she said. "You should ask her to come here to meet."

"Here!" Lorenzo said with some disdain. "Lake Haven, it is good for fishing. But not for true *amore.*"

"You're wrong, my friend. It's perfect," Jenny said, and handed the phone back to him. "There are no distractions here. No girlfriends to whisper in her ear. It's just you and her and the world as God gave it to us. No social media, no phones—"

Lorenzo gasped and grabbed her arm. "*Si,*" he said. "Yes, this is *brillante*, Jenny Turner. It is the only way. She *must* come here to me." He took a few steps away from her, one hand on top of his head, obviously thinking through the idea.

Jenny took another bite of her sandwich, her gaze finding Edan again. He was holding a pole now, his line cast. Fishing was such a solitary occupation.

"Now then, I will help you," Lorenzo announced.

Jenny's heart skipped. She looked up to see Lorenzo's smile of determination. "Umm…no thank you."

"No, I will not accept this. *I* know how a man's heart is won."

"That's great—but I'm not trying to win his heart," Jenny said, panicking a little. "I only want to be his friend."

"Friend! Men and women were not meant to be friends, Jenny Turner. There is only one way to bring him to you—you must make him jealous."

"No!" she exclaimed, horrified. "He's going back to his fiancée. Whatever you may think about it, he believes there's still a chance."

"Big mistake," Lorenzo said. "He mourns her yet. But mourning, it does not last forever. Loss lasts forever, but not grieves."

"Grief."

"What I mean, little peach, is that life goes on. But there are times that this life, it needs a bit of a push."

"Absolutely not," Jenny said, shaking her head, startled that Lorenzo had said the same thing her father had said all those years ago when her mother had died. He'd nudged her, all right, sending her off to school. *Life goes on,* he'd said. He'd been wrong about that at the time, because life didn't go on so easily, and to pretend it did had caused her to distrust her father.

She shook her head again. "I'm not going to bother him—"

"Bother? You will not *bother* him—he will want your more than air."

"No he won't—"

"Come," Lorenzo commanded.

"I don't want to."

Lorenzo bent over and took the sandwich from her hand and tossed it aside.

"Hey!"

He grabbed her wrist and pulled her to her feet, and with his thumb, knocked a crumb off her lip. He tilted his head to one side, studying her. He pulled her hair down from the top of her head, fluffed her bangs, and frowned a little. "It must do."

"Thanks a lot," Jenny snorted.

"Now then, we go."

"Lorenzo!" she cried as he gave her a sharp tug and made her march along with him down to the water's edge where Edan was fishing. "I don't want to do this!"

"Edan, my friend!" Lorenzo said, ignoring her. "You must show Jenny Turner how to do this fish."

Edan glanced over his shoulder at them, his gaze flicking over Jenny.

"You must teach her to cast the line," Lorenzo said loudly.

"Would you no' like to do it yourself, mate?" Edan asked, turning his attention back to his line.

Lorenzo nudged Jenny and winked at her. "Me? I am a fisherman, Eddy, not a teacher of children."

"Oh, *that's* nice," Jenny said as Lorenzo gave her a solid push toward Edan. Lorenzo dipped down to pick up a fishing rod, gave her a conspiratorial wink, then walked down the bank, away from them.

Jenny glanced at Edan. His expression was not what she would call warm and welcoming. He looked annoyed. "If you're to learn, you'll need to come here, to the water. You canna fish from the road."

"That's a slight exaggeration," she said. "I'm nowhere near the road."

"Aye, and you're nowhere near the lake."

"Fine," Jenny said. She picked her way over rocks and brush to the lake's edge.

"Well," Edan said.

"Well," Jenny repeated.

"Have you *ever* fished?"

"For a few compliments here and there, but never for an actual fish." She laughed at her jest.

"Mmm," he said. "Come on, then," he said, gesturing to the bank.

Jenny gingerly made her way closer.

"See the grasses there?" he asked, pointing with his tanned arm. "The larger fish will feed there. They are close to the shore here, aye? Fish are skittish, they are—donna talk and scare them off, aye?"

"Got it," she said. She wouldn't speak. She wouldn't move. She would catch her stupid fish and get out and let the poor man have his privacy.

His expression softened. "Aye, come on, then," he said, and held out his hand to her. Jenny slipped her hand into his. It felt warm and strong, and her heart fluttered a tiny bit. She allowed him to maneuver her to stand in front of him, which entailed some wobbling over rocks and brushing against the full length of him to avoid going into the lake before finding her footing. She was standing so close that she could feel his warmth at her back, the firm breadth of his chest. He put the rod in her hand, showed her how to work the reel, and then, holding her hand in his, showed her how to take the rod back and release the line.

"You want a bit of a rhythm before you cast, aye?" he said softly, and helped her draw her arm back and forth a few times before releasing the line. It sailed through the air and landed silently in the water.

"Nothing is happening," she whispered.

"Give it a wee bit," he said low into her ear, his breath warm on her cheek.

They stood, waiting.

"Maybe they know it's fake," she murmured. "I mean think about it—they've probably seen that same green and yellow thing a dozen times and they know that it always—"

Jenny was silenced when Edan put his hand over her mouth and whispered, *"Wheesht."*

She didn't know what that word meant, but it swept through her on a delightful little shiver. She decided he could say it to her whenever he liked.

Unfortunately, her silence did not result in a nibble. Edan helped her reel the line in, his body hard against her back, his arms strong around her. He helped her to cast again. And again.

The silence was killing her. Thoughts were churning in her head—more apologies for kissing him. Empathy for the way his engagement had ended. Questions about his life, his likes, his dislikes, his favorite TV show. Of her general tendency to rush in to things, like people's lives, like a bull in the proverbial china shop, and how she didn't want to do that and make everything worse.

"Remember the rhythm," he said, helping her to move her arm again.

Oh, she remembered it, all right. She remembered all sorts of rhythms and doubted she would ever forget this silent lesson. They threw the line and waited, one of his hands on her hip, the other covering her hand on the pole. "Quite a good cast, that was," he said.

"Really?"

"Aye. You could be a bloody good fisherman."

"I think I could learn to like it," she said. "I never really gave it a shot. I'm actually pretty bad about that, you know? Sometimes I don't give things—like jobs, for example—a real shot. And you know what else I do?" she said, a little frantically, all at once desperate to apologize for being so insensitive. "I assume things. I assumed that—"

"You're talking," he softly reminded her. "Donna scare them off."

"I'm sorry!" she suddenly blurted.

"It's all right, no harm done—"

"I'm such an *idiot*, kissing you in your kitchen like that and then telling you to get out more and talking about how lonely you are. I had no right."

"Jenny—"

"Even worse, I *know* what it's like to lose someone. Not exactly like you, but my mother died when I was ten. And I know how insensitive people can be about loss, because I feel like I've lost my father, but he's alive, and he's happy, and no one really gets it. But I do, and I never thought *I'd* be insensitive. I'm mortified that I—"

He suddenly cupped her chin and forced her head around to look at him. "Jesus, lass, it's all right. You've no' offended me. I am no' so tender I canna withstand a verra pleasant kiss from a verra bonny lass."

A lovely little shiver ran down her spine. "Okay, then," she said softly. "I mean, since you said I was bonny."

He pointed to her line. "Best keep your eyes out there."

Jenny glanced back at the sliver of line floating across the water. She didn't know what else to say to him. What more could possibly be said?

At that very moment, something jerked her line.

"I think you've got something, aye?" Edan said. His body surrounded hers, his arms shadowing hers, his chest, his legs, his groin, all pressed against hers in an effort to reel in whatever she'd caught. "Slowly, very slowly. Easy," he urged her.

"Ohmigod, it's a *fish*," she said, astonished that she'd caught anything.

"Donna get ahead of yourself, now. We've no' seen it—might very well be an old tire."

"Really?"

"No, no' really," he said, grinning. "Come on,

then, don't give any slack."

"She has one?" It was Lorenzo, somewhere behind them.

"I have one!" Jenny said excitedly.

"Slow," Edan warned her and, impossibly, shifted closer so that she was now smashed up against the full length of him. His head was just over her shoulder, his cheek brushing hers as he helped her reel it in. Her heart was pounding; she felt floaty and unsteady on her feet as she tried to do as he said and bring the fish in, while trying to ignore the sensation of every place they touched.

Lorenzo suddenly moved past her, splashing into the water and pulling up the line. At the end of it, a fish about six inches long was struggling.

"Huh," Jenny said. "That's it? I thought it was huge."

She could feel Edan's chuckle reverberating through him before he let her go.

"There's your supper," Lorenzo said.

"No, put it back," Jenny said.

Edan and Lorenzo exchanged a look.

"I can't *eat* him!" she exclaimed. "This is the same as catching one of those feral chickens under the Hollywood freeway. Everyone wants to catch them, but no one really wants to eat them."

The two men stared at her.

"Wait…you've never heard of the Hollywood chickens?"

Lorenzo sighed and handed the fish to Edan. Edan was smiling at Jenny. Actually smiling.

"The fishing, it is good," Lorenzo said. "Now, you come and give me your luck, no?" He stepped out of the lake and extended his hand for Jenny.

But she didn't want to leave. She wanted to fish with Edan. But Lorenzo had ruined the moment—Edan moved away from her to the water to cut the fish free.

"Come with me, Jenny Turner," Lorenzo said cheerfully, and threw his arm around her shoulders, giving her a hard squeeze before he forced her to march along with him once more.

He pulled her up onto the path that went around the lake and moved away from Edan. "That was so rude," she said.

"*Si*, very rude," Lorenzo blithely agreed. "And it will make this man crazy with want."

"I don't want to do that!" Jenny said, pushing away from Lorenzo.

"Don't be ridiculous. All the women want to make all the men crazy with want," he said, and winked at her.

Well. Maybe they did just a little. "Shut up," she said, and glanced back at Edan. He was casting his line again. He looked relaxed. In the zone. He did not look crazy with want. He looked quite content.

Jenny was the one who was crazy with want. She could still feel his body at her back, could still feel his breath on her cheek. She was falling. Tumbling, actually, cartwheeling down a hill for a Scottish guy she ought to leave the hell alone.

Twelve

———◆———

There was so much work to be done to close the inn, and Edan was terribly busy. Certainly too busy to concern himself with the coming and going of Jenny and that fucking Italian, as he'd come to think of Lorenzo. And yet, against his better judgment and true nature, Edan found ways to interrupt them. When he found them in the lounge bent over that blasted computer, he'd walked in and announced the internet service would be down for the afternoon.

"But this email is very important," Lorenzo pleaded with him, his palms together in a prayer pose.

"Sorry, lad. Canna be helped," Edan said, and had returned to his office and pulled the plug on the Wi-Fi.

When he saw them strolling along the road like lovers in springtime, he found reason to put himself in

Hugh's motorized mule and drive up to disrupt them. Jenny laughed brightly when he honked his horn and startled Lorenzo so badly that he jumped two feet in the air. "What is the reason for this horn!" Lorenzo demanded.

"To move dawdlers along," Edan said. "Looks like rain," he added, squinting up at the sky. "Shall I take you back to the inn?" He made certain that Jenny rode next to him, and Lorenzo in the cage in back.

And still he couldn't stop them. They are constantly whispering to each other and smiling. What could they possibly have to say to one another? They'd known each other for a whole of four days.

Edan realized, of course, that he'd somehow turned himself into a tragic mess. That kiss had taken on a life of its own in his head. As had the feel of her supple body against his.

He hated who he'd become these last few days. He hated that he was clinging to this idea of Audra who, really, when he thought about it, had shown him nothing but animosity in the last year. Oh sure, there had been sex and the dinners together, and quiet evenings—but there had always been an underlying current. And Edan was loyal to a fault, and he believed some things were worth fighting for, and he'd tried to make things right for her, tried to make Lake Haven up to her.

He should have known she'd hate this life. Audra had wanted a city, to be out of the Highlands. On his frequent trips home, Edan had convinced her and himself that she would be happy at Lake Haven.

She wasn't happy. It was Scotland all over again, except in America—too remote, too far from life.

He was distracted by these thoughts one

particularly sunny morning as he went out of the office to deliver paychecks. In the kitchen, he apparently was not responding appropriately to Rosalyn. She sighed and said, "You should take a few days off, Eddy. Go off and fish somewhere. You're overworked, aye?"

"Is that your subtle way of telling me you want me to leave your kitchen?"

"No. If I wanted you out of the kitchen I'd bloody well say it. I say it because you've been such a bear. I donna think you really want to close the inn."

Edan scowled as he handed her a paycheck. He walked out without a word because Rosalyn was right—he was disgusted with the world, feeling very uneasy in his skin, as if his parts weren't fitting together properly. He'd lost his center in the last week.

Ah, well, it would be over soon enough. Jenny had booked room 215 for another week after he'd pressed her. She'd be leaving, as would Lorenzo, as would the Pettimores. The last guests for the Cassian Inn.

His infatuation would fade when he got on a plane bound for Scotland.

If anything, that thought made him feel even more restless.

He stalked down to the farmhouse Ned and Sandra shared with his restlessness and foul mood and their paychecks. He entered the kitchen through the mudroom as he always did—and stopped midstride.

"Well, good morning!" Jenny said. She was up to her elbows in a mixing bowl and there was a splotch of flour on her cheek. She was wearing a dress, covered by Sandra's familiar apron, embroidered with a band of thistle around the edges.

It took a moment for Edan to make sense of what he was seeing and to check in with reality, and all the grand talk of how the infatuation would fade was smashed with a sledgehammer. "What are you doing here?" he asked.

"Making nut balls." She said it as if it were perfectly reasonable that she'd somehow found her way into Sandra's house and kitchen.

"Does Sandra know you are here, then?" he asked, confused.

Jenny laughed. "Of course she does. She invited me to use her kitchen. You don't want to hear it—it's a long story. Okay, I'll tell you. I had lunch in the restaurant yesterday, and I was dying for something sweet, but all Rosalyn had were these prepackaged cookies. And they were *awful*, Edan. Sorry to be the bearer of bad news, but *ick.* And you know how it is when you have your heart set on something sweet and find out it's no good? Anyway," she said, pausing to touch the back of her arm to her nose, "Sandra was there, and I said, 'You know what they say, sweets and porn are better when they're homemade,' and Sandra said she agreed about the sweets but didn't know about the porn, and neither do I, really, but you know, it's a joke, and we were talking, and one thing led to another, and I mentioned these delicious nut balls my mom used to make with butter and bourbon and pecans, and Sandra had all those things, and before you know it, she'd invited me over to make them for dinner tonight."

"But where—"

"She had to run up to the inn for something. Here, will you help me and put some of that wax paper down on the counter?" She smiled sweetly.

Edan cautiously stepped forward and did as she asked. As he stood there, Jenny scooped from the concoction in the bowl, balled it up in her hands, and placed them on the wax paper. "Hey, I was thinking," she said, and gave him a pert little smile. "Don't look so alarmed. I was thinking that you should have one of those little shops here so people can buy things from the inn. Like the chutney. You could put it in little mason jars and tie ribbons around it and sell it. Same for these nut balls. Really, if you think about it, you could make all kinds of stuff. Soap, pottery. Maybe even embroider some things. Sandra said she likes to embroider."

"You mean put in a tourist shop."

"A *farm* shop. They aren't the same thing. People really like the idea of getting organic food made right there, from ingredients found here."

"Aye, and who would manage this farm shop?" he asked as he slid onto a stool.

"Oh, you'd have to hire someone for sure. But the shop would pay for itself."

If only it were as simple as that.

"I really love homemade jellies and jams, and Sandra's jam is fabulous. And Rosalyn's pancake mix. Those two things alone could be a huge hit for you."

"We donna have space for mass production—"

"Sandra said she and your aunt talked about it once before." Jenny glanced up and gave him a sympathetic smile. "I'm so sorry about your aunt, by the way. Sandra said you two were very close."

"Aye, thank you. We were." Jenny and Sandra apparently had quite a long conversation.

"Well, anyway," Jenny said, resuming her work,

"she said they talked about it, but they weren't talking about a farm shop, exactly. They just wanted to make items for sale and put them in reception, but you were all like, *nooo,* we're a refined establishment." She arched a brow that challenged him to disagree as she walked to the fridge. She opened it, bent over, and began to rummage around in one of the lower drawers.

It hadn't exactly been like that, but any thought of correcting the record was dismissed as Edan admired her bum. He imagined it bare to him, smooth and soft and—

She popped up, closed the drawer with her foot and returned to the island with butter. "Do you remember?"

"Pardon?"

"That Sandra and your aunt talked to you about selling a few things."

Edan had to look away from her sparkling eyes in order to think. "Aye," he said. The reason he'd said no was because of Audra. She hadn't wanted to be bothered with it, and in order for the plan to work, they would have needed her help. "*I'm not a shop girl, Edan,*" she'd said with disdain.

"Would you mind—while I melt this butter, will you make some balls?"

The question sounded so ludicrous that one corner of Edan's mouth tipped up. "How can I refuse?" He walked around to her side of the island. She picked up some dough and put it in the palm of his hand, then closed his fingers over it. She glanced up through her lashes, and her eyes, bloody hell, they were shining with desire, prompting an unwelcome surge of lust through him. "Just make a little ball," she said, squeezing his fingers a bit. "Then roll it in this bowl." She pointed to one that was filled with a powdery substance. "And put it here," she ended, pointing to the wax paper.

"That's all?" he asked her.

Her lips curved. "That's all...for now," she said, her voice sounding almost like a purr to him. And then she moved away.

Edan began to make the balls while she tended the melting butter. "You're a cook, then," he said.

"Sort of. When I was fifteen, I took a cooking class because I was worried Dad wouldn't eat properly. I liked baking the best. I learned to make pies and cakes and flans, and brownies and muffins...well, you get the picture."

"Your father must have been greatly appreciative," Edan said.

"Maybe, but it didn't last long," she said with a shrug. "Our kitchen wouldn't have passed anyone's health inspection and the baking pans I bought were buried under some other stuff."

Edan tried to imagine the kitchen of a hoarder. He tried to imagine how Jenny had survived in that environment.

Jenny shifted away from the stove to check his progress, her caramel head bending over the bowl. "And I don't bake much now, because if I baked for a party of one, I'd blow up like that blowfish Hootie."

"Hootie and the Blowfish is a band," Edan said. "No' a fish."

"Hmmm?" She looked up, her gaze meeting his. "I'm pretty sure it's a blowfish."

"Nope. No' a fish," he said, his gaze moving over her pretty face.

"You seem pretty firm about it," she said, and her lips curved into a smile.

"Some things a man canna let slide," he muttered. There was an invitation in her eyes, an invitation that sizzled between them, a palpable current as smooth and as hot as the butter melted in the pan. Edan didn't know what possessed him, but this time, he was the one who was doing the kissing. She was in his arms, and he was tracing the seam of her lips with the tip of his tongue. He dug his fingers into the soft flesh of her hips, pulling her into his body. He caught her jaw and tilted her head so that he could draw her bottom lip between his teeth before slipping his tongue into her mouth.

Jenny's hands slipped up his chest, to his neck and his hair, and her leg came up, sliding along his thigh. He caressed the bare skin above the bodice of her dress and could feel her heart beating against his palm, could feel the warmth of her skin. He moved his hand to her breast, kneading it, then followed the path of his hand with his mouth, sliding his mouth down her chin, to the hollow of her throat, then the swell of her breast. He closed his eyes to the storm brewing in him and allowed himself to feel. No thinking, just feeling. Her skin, her breath, the curve of her body— everything.

The sound of voices outside reached them at the same time. Edan lifted his head and glanced at the door. He sighed, calmly helped her arrange her dress and apron. Jenny was a little more frantic about it, but surprisingly quiet for once. He cupped her chin, and she sighed, her eyes half closed, as he nipped at her lips once more. He then walked out of the kitchen, grabbing up a nutball as he went, and left via the front door.

When Edan stepped outside, he paused to look at the sky overhead and breathe in a deep drink of fresh air. It felt like the first bit of fresh air he'd felt in his lungs in an age—he could almost feel the cobwebs lifting away. His body was thrumming—every nerve, every muscle alive and ready. He hadn't wanted sex like this since—

"Eddy, my friend!"

Edan jumped and jerked around at the sound of Lorenzo's voice.

"A beautiful day! We will play today some golf, yes?" Lorenzo waved as he carried on to the mudroom door and disappeared inside the farmhouse.

Edan's blood went from simmering to pure boil.

Thirteen

Jenny was still rooted to the very spot where Edan had kissed her when Lorenzo peeked in the back door. He stepped in and looked at her with alarm. Maybe because she wasn't breathing. She was absolutely, completely breathless.

"What is wrong?" he exclaimed.

"He *kissed* me," she said, her voice still fluttery with excitement. "I don't even know how it happened—"

"*Brava, brava!*" Lorenzo said, clapping as he walked to the kitchen island, pausing momentarily to help himself to a nutball. "You see? My plan, it is very smart. You are in love?"

"No!" Jenny said, and then laughed nervously. She sounded like a hyena.

"But of course you are—this is *amore* at its best,

no?"

She swatted his hand away from the nutballs. That's when she noticed several of them had been smashed. She probably had nutball all over her ass. "You're way ahead of yourself, buddy," she said, and poured the melted butter into the batter and stirred.

"Why do you wound me, Jenny Turner? I am an expert in the heart's affairs."

"Oh sure. That's why things are going so well between you and Elizabetta."

"But I loved her the moment my eyes saw her."

"Then why did you kiss someone else?" Jenny asked as she began to make more nutballs.

"I am a man of many appetites, little peach. That was an indiscretion," he said with a dismissive flick of his wrist. "Elizabetta is my one and only love."

Jenny laughed at him. She was as giddy as a damn schoolgirl. "I think your eye wouldn't wander quite so much if that were true."

"I am a man," he said grandly. "When my eye no longer wanders, I am dead. I knew I was certain Elizabetta would be mine the moment she desired to have a leather handbag that to me looked like every other handbag," he said, making a sweeping gesture. "But no—*this* handbag was the *only* handbag she would have. No other would do." He leaned forward and locked his gaze on Jenny's. "It was a priceless handbag. I could give her a house for this price. But I gave her this handbag that looked like all the others, for it is the one that made her happy. *That*, Jenny Turner, is when I knew."

Jenny smiled. "That's actually so romantic, Lorenzo."

He touched the tip of her nose. "Sometimes, the

heart knows and keeps the secret from the brain," he said, touching her forehead.

She slapped his hand away. "Will you stop? It's like walking around in a romance novel with you. Have you heard from Elizabetta today?"

Lorenzo's demeanor instantly changed. "No," he said, and sat on a stool, propped up his head with his fist. "She does not love me as I love her. She does not wish me to be happy."

They had sent a new email just last night, entreating Elizabetta a second time to come to Lake Haven.

"But now, we think not of me, but of you, Jenny Turner. Now is the time to catch the fish. Now is the time we—"

"Hold it right there," she said, holding up a spatula. "I think we've taken the jealousy thing far enough. I'll take it from here."

"*You?*" He laughed roundly. "You know nothing of this. You are *bambino* when it comes to the heart. I have a plan—"

"No plans!" Jenny said firmly. "Whatever happens, happens. It's bad karma to interfere with fate. Sometimes, you have to go with the flow."

Lorenzo sighed. "All my hard work, and you will toss it away like a bothersome feather." He swiped another nutball and munched it sorrowfully. "Remember, Jenny Turner, if Eddy thinks you pursue him, he will run like the fox."

"I'm not *pursuing* him," she insisted. She didn't know what exactly she was doing, but she didn't want Lorenzo orchestrating anything. She would work it out herself. Except that she had no plan for how to proceed with Edan. None whatsoever. But she had a plan! It was a different plan, and where Edan fit into it, who knew? She had to let the chips fall where they may.

She'd talked to her dad last night. He'd enthusiastically encouraged her to pursue her idea, to bring him some information. So she'd casually spoken to a Realtor this morning in a fact-finding mode. Jenny was determined to go for it, to buy this inn. The desire was growing in her every moment.

She was still mulling it over later that evening after the dining room had closed and Lorenzo had gone off in search of a pub, and she'd decided to take advantage of a perfectly lovely summer's evening to walk off the generous portion of Scottish salmon and potatoes she'd had. And a few too many nutballs, if she was being honest.

She'd made it to the top of the hill when her phone began to jingle in her pocket. "Hi Vanessa," she said when she answered.

"Hello, Jennerator," Vanessa said cheerfully. "Still feeling the magic out there in the hinterlands?"

Jenny smiled thinly. "If you called to lecture me—"

"I didn't! I am calling to talk to you about a job!"

She announced it as if Jenny had just won the *Reader's Digest* sweepstakes.

"I have these clients with a chain of coffee shops. Morning Joes, they're called. They just opened one in Santa Monica, and they are looking for management staff. So I told them about you and guess what. They're interested."

"Wow," Jenny said.

"You'd be perfect for it, Jenny," Vanessa said enthusiastically. "You're so good with people. And you have such a creative mind. I know you could think of ways to bring in business."

"What, like classes on existentialism in the evenings or something like that?" Jenny tossed out there.

"Well, maybe not that class exactly, but yes, creative," Vanessa said.

Jenny was only half joking. That actually sounded like a great idea. She could do something like that here, on the first tee. "Thanks, Vanessa. I really appreciate it."

"Of course, they'll have to vet you. I told them you're on sabbatical and I made it sound fancy, because that's what I do for my friends. And they said sure, of course. But I don't think you can hang out there forever if you're interested. When should I tell them you'll be back?"

"About that," Jenny said, and squeezed her eyes shut a moment. "I'm not sure I'll be back."

That was met with silence. And then, "Why?"

"Because I am thinking of buying this inn," Jenny said, plunging right in. "It's going on the market soon."

"*What?*" Vanessa cried. "Are you crazy?"

"I don't think so," Jenny answered honestly.

"Jenny!" Vanessa said sternly, and proceeded with the harangue Jenny knew she'd get from all her friends. Vanessa pointed out how ill-equipped Jenny was to take on an inn, that she knew nothing about running a business, how flighty she could be in most things, and how she could not simply quit an inn she'd bought if she didn't like it.

When she'd finished, or had paused to take a breath, Jenny didn't know, as she'd stopped listening,

Jenny said with a calmness she didn't feel, "Thanks for you concern, V. Seriously. I know you mean well, but this time, I know what I'm doing."

"Oh, Jenny," Vanessa said wearily, as if Jenny were the child who continued to disappoint her.

Jenny felt teary all of a sudden. She had the best friends in the world—but they were wrong about her. She bit back her tears and said, "Love you, man."

Vanessa sighed. "Love you, man," she returned softly.

Jenny slid the phone into her pocket and began a slow walk back to the inn. Her head was full of the conflict of doubts and the steady drum of confidence that this was right. It was a huge thing for her to do, and it was true she had no track record of doing huge things. But there was always a first time, wasn't there? Something had brought her to this inn. Something had drawn her to Edan Mackenzie, something deeper than a surface infatuation. This place, and that man beckoned her soul.

It sounded insane, even to her. But Jenny believed, and while it very well might be insane, it didn't mean she didn't feel it any less.

What Edan felt about her, she couldn't say. And she couldn't concern herself with it—whatever happened, the most important thing was that she was true to herself.

At the moment she had that thought, the sun divided the clouds and Edan emerged from the wooded path that she now knew led up to his aunt's grave. Jenny stopped walking. This was true serendipity.

He looked up and paused on the path just ahead of her. "Jenny?"

"Hi," she said, and waved a little. She took a cautious step forward. "Nice evening."

"Aye." His expression was soft. Slightly affectionate.

"So umm…" She could suddenly hear Lorenzo in her head, warning her not to pursue him. So she said, "I was hoping I'd run into you." Forget Lorenzo.

"Were you?" He smiled warmly.

"I want to ask you something."

"Aye, and what is that?"

Good question, Outlander. Jenny took another step forward. "I wanted to ask about lodging. Not for me. For others. Like, how is it?"

His brows dipped. "I donna understand."

She drew a breath. She'd never been good at beating around a bush. "I guess I should come right out and say it. I'm thinking of buying the inn."

He looked stunned. "You're *what*?"

"I'm thinking of buying your inn." She smiled hopefully.

He shoved his hands into his pockets as she took another step toward him. "*This* inn," he said, as if there were dozens to choose from.

"This one."

One of his dark brows slowly arched above the other. She was struck by the amazing shine of his eyes in the waning light of day. So deep, so sexy, so full of want. Granted, that might be a bit of projecting on her part, but still.

"It's no' easy, managing an inn," he said.

"I know. Well, I assumed. But I will learn. I really *want* to learn."

He nodded. His eyes moved over her. "We should talk about it, aye?"

Jenny nodded.

He gestured to the path. Jenny pulled her sweater tighter around her and began to walk with him.

She sucked at this, the silent strolling. She could imagine if they were married for fifty years, she'd still feel that insane urge to talk at moments like this. "I had the most amazing salmon tonight," she said, apropos of nothing.

"Ah."

"I thought you'd be interested. Since you love fishing so much, you know. I am finally getting why someone would like to fish. It's thrilling when you actually catch something, and honestly, I feel a little enlightened. You know how it is, you go along in life thinking that you really hate something, like brussels sprouts, and you are so convinced that you hate brussels sprouts that you begin to believe you must hate them because they give you hives or something, and then one day, you end up eating brussels sprouts and they're *delicious*, and you think hey…why did I think I hated brussels sprouts?" She looked at him. "That's fishing."

"Interesting theory," he said, his eyes, which were deep sea green now and shining with amusement.

Jenny imagined a tiny version of herself getting on a tiny boat to explore the sea of Edan. "Is it?" she murmured.

He smiled and took her elbow, steering her to the left. "No."

He escorted her to the back of the inn, and into his quarters, through the kitchen, and into a room with soaring ceilings. It was tastefully furnished with overstuffed chairs, a thick, shaggy rug, and built-in cases stuffed full with books. This is exactly how she would have pictured his living space.

He carried on, to an adjoining office. The windows in here were as tall as the ceiling, completely unadorned, and framing a spectacular view of the woods and the lake. His desk was very neat—nothing but his laptop, a stack of papers in a tray, and a single pen. Were it not for a pair of men's shoes kicked to one side, she would think he never used this room.

Jenny had an image of him on a cold winter night, all alone, surfing the internet and giving in to flash sales on fishing poles.

Edan went to a small table and opened a crystal decanter. "Whisky?" Jenny shook her head. He poured himself a finger of whisky, and then turned around to face her. "Might I ask what made you think to purchase the inn?"

Jenny looked around the paneled walls, the thick beamed ceiling overhead. How many years had this house stood here? How many ghosts had slipped in and out of its walls? She couldn't wait to find out. She couldn't wait to learn everything there was about it. "I don't know. I feel drawn to it. I feel like this is where I belong."

He sipped the whisky. "Have you any notion of what it entails, running an inn?"

"You mean besides what I googled last night? No."

He glanced down at his glass, as if considering his words. When he looked up he said, "It's no' something you do on the fly, Jenny—"

"Stop," Jenny said, holding up her hand. She would hear the speech she knew was coming from everyone else, but she did not want to hear it from

Edan. Anyone but him. "Look, Edan, I know how I come across. I know I seem like I flit around like a hummingbird. But I've needed something for a very long time, and I think I've found it. I've spent the last nineteen years arranging my life around someone who didn't need me in the end. When my dad told me to go get my own life, it made me realize that I have forgotten how to think about what I need. I'm doing that now. So I can't explain why now, or why here. I can only tell you that I *feel* it, and I feel it strongly. I need this and I have confidence in me even if no one else does."

Several moments of silence ticked by. Edan was looking at her intently, and Jenny resisted the urge to fidget. She knew what he thought. He thought she was silly. Impetuous. Maybe he even thought she was dumb.

"I understand," he said softly. He put his glass aside. "I completely understand forgetting to think about what you need."

He said nothing more than that, and they stood for a moment, looking at each other. She wondered if he was waiting for her to say good night. Whatever he was thinking, Jenny's spirit was once again unwilling to let the silence just be. "I'm going to sell the nutballs at the inn."

His eyes wandered over her, and her hair, which she'd left loose to dry after her bath, down her dress and sweater, to her legs, to her feet and her sandals. His gaze was hot. Intent. And it lit a furnace in her.

"I brought them to the dining room and they were a big hit," she said, her voice sounding a little weird to her. "Everyone was talking about them. *These nutballs are amazing*," she said, mimicking the voice of a crowd.

Edan reached for her hand and pulled her closer.

"If they go that crazy over nutballs, imagine what they'd do with my red velvet cake."

He cupped her face with his hands. "Imagine," he muttered, and kissed her.

If there was one thing that could make Jenny shut up, it was a great kiss and the prospect of great sex. She sank into Edan. Something had shifted between them, as if they'd come to an unspoken mutual agreement—they were into each other. At least sexually—she wasn't going to overthink it. Jenny was firmly planted in the headspace of letting fate come to her. She was going to go with the flow, and the flow was hot and sexy.

She could feel the heat of his body through his shirt, could feel her own blood rising to the surface. He touched her hair, pulling his fingers through it, and then slid his hand around her nape.

Jenny began to lose sense of time and where she was, exactly. She was completely submerged in the electric sensations of his hands and his mouth on her body. He touched her everywhere—her breasts, between her legs, her arms, her hips. His lips were both soft and demanding and tormented her, making her blood rush hot in her veins.

He moved down her body, his mouth on her abdomen as he flipped off one sandal, and then the other. He slowly rose back up, his hands trailing behind his mouth. They were moving, Jenny realized, and her sweater had come off. There were too many articles of clothing between them, too many fabrics, and she was grabbing at his shirt, pulling it from his trousers, her fingers running up the buttons. When she at last had his shirt undone and off his body he paused and regarded her with his deep, sea-green eyes.

"My God, Edan. You're gorgeous," she said.

He ran his hand roughly over her head. "What a bonny lass you are," he said.

Jenny melted. She was an aroused lass, too.

They kept moving, lips and hands on each other, until Jenny realized they were in a bedroom. He had a platform bed and his things were scattered about. A pair of shoes, some jeans draped over a chair. A tray on the dresser where a few bills were visible. Two dog beds, which had been inhabited by two dogs until he shooed them out and shut the door.

He turned around to her and took her in. He pushed her disheveled hair behind her ear, stroked her chin. "I am surprised by you," he said softly. "You were the last thing I expected to arrive at the inn, aye? And yet, here you are."

She reached for his belt. "You surprised me, too. I was expecting a gramps-and-grandma kind of operation. Not a man in a kilt."

He kissed her. "I want you, Jenny," he whispered into her ear. "I want you in a way I didna think possible."

The throaty way he uttered those words spiraled through her and erupted into tiny little explosions of light inside her. "I want you, too—"

"I donna want to interfere with the path you are exploring, but I canna help but ask if you're certain this is what you want."

She kissed his face, his neck. "I am more than certain. Don't you want to lose those pants?"

"I mean the inn, aye? This life."

"The inn is literally the furthest thing from my

mind right now," she said, and slipped her hands around his waist.

"It can be a solitary life, aye? There are days, particularly in the winter, that seem so long without a body to keep you warm. I want you to have someone, Jenny. I want you to feel needed and loved—"

"Edan, seriously, you're finally going to talk *now*?" she asked, and threw her arms around his neck and kissed him.

Edan caught her waist, twirled her around, and threw them both onto the bed. Jenny giggled at the bit of bouncing they did.

"There is quite a lot I have to say about your alarming idea," he said, and began to move down her body, rolling her to one side to unzip her dress. "But I suppose it can wait." He shimmied the dress down her body, and Jenny's laughter began to fade into panting.

He bit at her panties, dragging them down her body with his teeth. He expertly removed her bra, then traced her body with his hands in one long caress. Jenny felt as if she'd been starved for weeks, and he was the sustenance she needed. Jenny could feel his racing pulse beneath her lips, the muscles working in his back and hips as he explored her body. He kissed and stroked her, arousing her to delirious pleasure, and just when she thought she'd have to beg, he fumbled in a bedstand for a condom.

She was beside herself with desire, and when he rolled onto his back and put her on top, Jenny was eager to move things along. She began to move on him, sliding up and down his erection.

But Edan put his hands on her hips and slowed her. "You've really caught me by surprise, aye?"

"That's what you said," she breathlessly agreed,

and tried to maneuver herself onto his cock.

"It must be true that lightning strikes when you're least—"

"Edan!" she said, and leaned over him, her hair spilling around them. "Stop *talking*," she said, and silenced him with a deep kiss.

He returned her kiss with one that was hard and full of purpose and passion and need. He began to move with her and slid solidly into her body. Jenny gasped with pleasure. She was lost from that moment, riding along as Edan captained the ship.

Edan abruptly flipped her onto her back, draped one of her legs over his shoulder, and tenderly caressed her face as he moved in her, reverently kissing her lips and her skin. Jenny had never felt more desirable to a man in her life. Her response to his attention built to an explosion, catapulting her into pure ecstasy, a release so spectacular that she was certain none would ever compare again.

Edan's release was just as explosive; he came with a deep groan of satisfaction. When he stilled, he covered her face with breathless kisses and carefully rolled off of her to lay beside her, tangling his fingers with hers as he sought his breath. Jenny was gulping for air, too, but she felt as if she were still soaring high above them.

"Magical," Edan said.

Magical. His choice of word thrilled her, because that is exactly what she would have said. It *was* magical.

"And I donna say so lightly. I've been hiding from truth for too long now. I'll no' hide any longer."

Jenny opened her eyes and blinked. What truth was he talking about?

"I suppose I get caught up in the work like everyone, aye?" He stroked her hair, twined some of it around a finger. "I've been thinking about the back of the inn. Seems as good a good place as any for a terrace and maybe an outdoor bar."

He'd been thinking about it? Did that mean he wanted to stay? Jenny's heart began to patter a little harder. She rolled onto her side, propped herself up on her elbow and stared down at him.

"We'd have little use of it in winter, but in the summer, it would be bonny. There's the cottage at the end of the lane, as well," he mused as he brushed the tip of a tress of her hair across her collarbone. "Clara thought it would make a good honeymoon suite."

"Who *are* you?" she asked. "You've said more in the last half hour than you have all week."

He smiled at her.

She smiled back. She was probably letting her emotions run wild, but Jenny felt like something profound had happened to her. Like a secret door had opened and warm, bright light had come streaming in. She could feel every single beat of her heart; she could feel the emotions churning. Everything was different for her this time. Edan, this inn—all of it.

"There's an inn in the Hamptons that I'd like to see. It's got quite an excellent reputation," he said, and began to talk about improvements that he thought could be made to the Cassian Inn.

She discovered she loved listening to him talk. She loved his Scottish brogue, she loved the feel of him next to her. She loved planning a future, hearing him talk about the things that made her indescribably happy. She buried herself into his side and listened. It was like he'd finally unlocked the gates and miscellaneous thoughts and ideas were rushing out. Jenny understood completely. He'd at last pushed past the trauma of his broken engagement. He was ready to take part in the world again.

But it turned out that even Jenny had her limits. When Edan began to talk about the maintenance required for the golf course, she had to silence him with a kiss. And more. Much more. She learned something else that night—she was not the only one who was made mute by great sex.

By the time sleep overtook her, Jenny was happy and sated, both emotionally and physically. She'd reached across an invisible divide and had brought Edan to her side. She ought to have a tiara, one that indicated she was the queen of perception and understanding of others. A tiara with lots of diamonds, she thought sleepily as she began to drift away.

She was feeling quite content when she awoke the next morning.

The sun streamed in through the windows of Edan's room, and Jenny smiled and rolled onto her back, stretching long…but the sheets were cool. She rolled onto her side.

Edan was not here.

She sat up and looked around. He was not in the bathroom, as the door was standing open and the light was off. She got up, found most of her clothes, and padded into his office in search of her sandals.

As she looked around, she heard Edan in the kitchen and walked in there, prepared to give him a big smoochy kiss. He was standing behind the kitchen island with a cup of tea in his hand, and he smiled when she came in. "Morning."

But Jenny's heart stopped beating. She knew

instantly that something had changed. Chatty Cathy had disappeared, and stoic, quiet, Edan Mackenzie had returned. He was already dressed for the day in slacks and shirt and tie. And there were her sandals and her sweater, folded and stacked neatly on one of the kitchen chairs.

She was being sent on her way. Jenny couldn't believe it—the magic of last night was dissipating like fog in sun, and she was being sent on her fucking way. She wasn't sure what to do—she hadn't imagined the connection between them. "Good morning," she said, and slid her arms, loosy-goosy, across the kitchen island, playfully reaching for him.

He leaned down and kissed her forehead. Her *forehead.*

Jenny slowly rose up. Maybe she should have been angry, but she actually felt a little sorry for Edan that he couldn't seem to get out of his own damn way.

Or was he a fox, like Lorenzo had warned her? Was he escaping what he saw were her clutches? But she'd felt such profound things last night, and dammit, so had he!

Her confusion turned to anger, but Jenny had her pride, and she wasn't going to let him see her disappointment. Right now, the only thing she could think about was getting out of here without slinking.

"Tea?" he asked.

"No thank you. No time for that," she said cheerfully. "I've got a lot to do today." She grabbed her sandals and slid them on, then picked up her sweater. "Looks like a great day. Not a cloud in the sky!" She walked around the kitchen island and rose up and kissed him on the cheek. "Thanks for last night. That's just what the doctor ordered—fantastic sex."

Edan looked down at his teacup and Jenny had the sense he was suddenly searching for words. Maybe he'd expended his weekly allotment last night. Maybe he was truly at a loss. And maybe he was like every other guy who was in it just for the sex—he didn't know how to tell her that's all it had been. See? This was precisely why a woman needed non-negotiables! Just one other thing her friends were right about.

"Hey, don't look serious," she said, truly furious now. "Not everything is so *serious*." She smiled, patted his cheek, and made herself walk to the kitchen door and out onto the terrace. She had to force herself not to run like she wanted, because she could feel his eyes on her. But what she really wanted was to flee to some distant corner of the earth and nurse her wounds.

Fourteen

———◆———

So much for going with the flow.

Jenny returned at a clip to room 215, showered, and changed her clothes. Her confusion and disappointment had burgeoned into raw anger. With herself, with Edan, with the fact that she always believed things would be different and they rarely were. When would she learn?

She grabbed a hat, some shades, her jacket and her yoga mat, and went outside.

All right. He was a jerk in a long line of them. If only she could convince herself it had been only a roll in the hay for him. She couldn't. No matter how she tried to rationalize it, last night had meant something to him, she was certain, but he was an ass and wouldn't admit it, even to himself. Idiot.

That didn't mean Jenny wasn't going to buy this

inn. She was. Edan had not dampened her enthusiasm for the inn. It was only growing. He could go back to Scotland to a woman who didn't want him. And besides, Jenny really didn't have time for Edan anyway. She had a lot to sort through and learn and do. She would chalk this up to what it apparently was—sex with a man who loved his ex and needed to release a pent-up need. And she had no one but herself to blame because she had started it with that kiss. So she would also chalk it up to *fantastic* sex and look forward.

She walked for a very long time before she felt calm enough to roll out her mat. She glanced at the pendant watch she wore—she'd been walking for two and a half hours.

Jenny went through her yoga practice, then sat cross-legged on her mat, her eyes closed, her hands together in prayer pose, and listened to the sound of nature around her. She prayed for understanding and compassion, and a smooth transition to this new life.

By the time she stood up and rolled up her mat, she was calmer and centered. She knew how this thing with Edan would end. She would be the bigger person, of course. She imagined herself knocking on his door with a basket of nutballs. She would calmly explain they were her parting gift. She would say she was happy to have made his acquaintance and a Realtor would soon be in touch. He would thank her and take her nutballs.

And then she imagined him falling on his knees and begging her to forgive him. Jenny starred in this version. She caressed his head and remind him that it was better this way, that he was so piteously desperate for a woman who had dumped him that she wouldn't feel right if he didn't get on with it and get out.

Oh, who was she kidding? There weren't any nutballs left.

Jenny returned to the inn, her mind on the paperwork the Realtor said she'd need to proceed.

"Jenny!"

Vanessa's voice startled her so completely that she jerked around and dropped her yoga mat, because Vanessa and Brooke were standing near the entrance.

Jenny picked up her yoga mat. "What the hell? What are you doing here?"

"What do you think?" Brooke asked cheerfully. "We came to check on you."

"*What?* Why?"

"Don't get upset," Vanessa said. "It's Friday and I've never been to Lake Haven. And it's not every day one of my besties buys an inn. I wanted to see it."

Brooke chucked Jenny on the shoulder. "Which way to the bar?"

"It's eleven a.m., Brooke. And there is no bar. And the inn isn't really open for business."

"Which is why we booked rooms at the resort on the north shore," Vanessa said. "They have a bar. And a *spa.*" She rubbed her hands together as if she'd just stumbled on a bag of diamonds.

"So let's go there," Brooke said.

"I have to change," Jenny said. "I'll be back in a minute." She left her friends admiring the roses in the courtyard and hurried inside to change.

Fifteen minutes later, they were in the SUV Vanessa had rented, driving around the lake.

At the resort, Vanessa and Brooke checked into a plush room, and then the three of them headed to the bar and took a table near the windows. When they'd ordered their drinks and some food, Brooke folded her arms on the table, looked at Jenny and said, "Okay. What's really up with this inn business, Jen?"

"Nothing," Jenny said with a shrug. In a most curious twist of her universe, for the first time in a very long time, she did not want to talk about it.

"Nothing? Seriously? You've been here a weekend and you're buying the place? It's a little nutty, even for you."

"Actually, it's been almost two weeks," she said, as if that would make a great difference. "And so what if I am? You guys are so desperate for me to get a job. This is a job."

"I was thinking of a job you might know a little about. You don't know anything about running an inn," Vanessa pointed out.

"I'll learn," Jenny said irritably. "Why are you so against it?"

"I'm not," Vanessa said calmly.

"She's not!" Brooke said, less calmly. "*We're* not. But you have to admit, you have a tendency to be really impetuous."

"I admit I can be really impetuous," Jenny conceded. "But I can also be pretty dedicated. You didn't even look at the inn. You didn't see what I saw."

"Okay," Vanessa said. "Fair point. But if you're so down with this idea, then why do you look so sad?"

"I look sad? I don't look sad. I'm *not* sad," she insisted.

"You look *totally* sad," Brooke said.

Jenny waved her hand at Brook and averted her gaze. "I'm tired, that's all." She was completely and utterly exhausted, she realized. *Emotionally* exhausted. It was weighing her down. Jenny was pretty good about keeping her spirits up, but even she could admit that the last few months had been a roller coaster, and after last night... Jenny didn't realize she was slowly sinking into her chair until her forehead rested on the table.

"Ohmigod," Vanessa said. "Hello!" she called to the waitress. "We need another round over here!"

Jenny slowly lifted her head and propped it up on her palm. "I slept with someone."

"*Who?*" Brooke demanded.

"The owner of the inn. Same guy I kissed."

"Oh, that guy," Vanessa said. "Well, okay. Maybe it helped you forget Devin."

Jenny snorted. "I forgot Devin the day I left him."

"Was it bad?" Brooke asked, wrinkling her nose.

"No! It was outstanding."

"Then why so sad?" Vanessa asked, looking befuddled.

"I really like him," Jenny said. "I *really* do. He's quiet, and he's sort of a loner, and there is something about him that really speaks to me. Unfortunately, he's not over his ex."

"Why?" Brooke asked. "Did it just happen?"

"A few months ago, I think."

Brooke leaned back, frowning.

"The sex was freaking *awesome*," Jenny said. "All the bells and whistles went off. I even *congratulated* myself on facilitating his entry back into living after a bad breakup."

Vanessa laughed.

"Sadly, I'm not kidding," Jenny said somberly. "But this morning, it was clear he was having second thoughts." She threw up her hands. "Story of my life."

"That is so *not* the story of your life," Brooke scoffed.

"It is. When I find a man I'm really interested in, it always turns out that they are not so interested in me. They want someone thinner and prettier and blonder. They want *you.*"

"No they don't," Brooke scoffed, and flipped the ends of her platinum-blonde hair over her shoulder.

"I'm used to it, but this felt a lot different to me. It almost felt like…like…" Her gut was twisting.

"Like what?" Vanessa pressed her. "Love?"

The word startled Jenny. "Sort of. Like he needs me. There, I said it. It felt so different because I think he really needed me. *Needs* me. But I don't think he knows it."

"If this guy doesn't see you for the wonderful, beautiful person you are, then it's his loss," Vanessa said.

"The thing is, I thought maybe he did see something more to me. Not at first, because I know it takes a bit to warm up to me. Remember in college how awful Professor Trewillier was to me for the first few weeks? But once he got to know me, he liked me, remember? It was kind of like that. I thought Edan was really starting to like me, and maybe he does, but he obviously likes this chick in Scotland more. He told me this week he loved her."

Brooke and Vanessa exchanged a look. "Who knows, Jen," Brooke said. "It's hard to know anyone in the space of a few days. Maybe your timing is all wrong. Maybe he just needed more time to get over it. And you always say, if it's meant to be, it will be." She shrugged, picked up her drink, and sipped. "You must be rubbing off on me because I actually believe that," she said, and clinked her glass against Jenny's.

"Forget him," Vanessa said cheerfully. "Let's go look at this inn."

For Edan, the day had flown by in a whirl of emotion and work. The morning stayed with him, shadowing his every move like a dog. He didn't think he'd ever forget standing at the kitchen window, watching Jenny walk across his terrace, her dress swinging around her knees in a carefree manner, while he'd been reeling. Had it truly been such a casual thing to her? Another day, another shag?

He'd turned away from the window, full of tender feelings for Jenny Turner. So tender that he was thinking of drastic things.

Edan considered himself to be a generally measured, thoughtful man. He planned things. He thought things through, considered all sides. He did not make decisions on a whim. He did *not* make decisions on the basis of how good the sex had been.

But he was about to.

It wasn't just the sex, really—it was the way his thoughts were warring with his emotions. His common sense was trying to convince him that he was experiencing euphoria from sex after a long absence from it, while the devil was whispered into his heart— was *still* whispering, goddammit—that Jenny was someone entirely different from any woman he'd ever known. Based on nothing other than a feeling. But that feeling went straight to the core of him.

He'd decided things in the light of dawn when he'd glanced down, seen her caramel hair covering her face, sprawled across his bed and taking up every inch of spare space with her limbs bent and splayed across it. He'd been aroused and he'd wanted her again, but he'd also needed to think about what the hell he was doing, so he'd eased himself out of bed.

He'd showered, dressed, made tea. He'd thought all sorts of things, millions of things in that time— mostly big-picture things, like how he was entitled to live his life. That he had nothing left to prove. That he'd actually bought into her ideas for the inn, because he'd had similar thoughts through the years.

That he very much liked it here at Lake Haven and always had. The inn was a challenge and always would be. And he meant it when he said it wasn't the sort of place you wanted to end up alone, especially in winter. What he needed was a partner. Call him crazy, but he thought that partner could be Jenny.

Aye, then, crazy. You've known her for the space of a few days and between the sheets, and now you're thinking of how bonny it would be to run an inn with her?

That's what he'd been thinking when she'd bounded out of his room this morning, all cheerful and flushed. Edan had to work not to panic, because the craziness was particularly strong when he looked at her. But then she'd rushed off as if she'd finished her laundry and needed to get to the next task.

It had left him feeling quite vulnerable.

Nevertheless, he'd gone on to work as men do, just as he always went to work when Audra was unhappy. He'd seen the Pettimores off and had closed that account, then had closed the door of his office and tried to concentrate on the mounds of paperwork he'd let slide as he'd worked to close the inn.

He'd lost track of time when Rosalyn poked her head in his office. "You canna go without food, lad. You'll make yourself ill." She presented him a plate of fish and chips.

"Thank you," he muttered, and pretended to be concentrating on his work.

But Rosalyn lingered. She wandered over to the window, from where she could see the front drive and courtyard. "Ah, there's Jenny and her friends," she announced.

Edan assumed Rosalyn meant Lorenzo and perhaps his brothers. "Friends," he repeated.

"Aye. Girlfriends come up from the city."

Now he glanced up. "We're no' open. I've no rooms ready for them."

"They're staying at the resort," Rosalyn said.

"Of course they are," he said a little darkly. That resort had been the bane of this inn. It was impossible for quaint to compete with luxury amenities.

"Tsk tsk, Eddy. In a mood again, are you?" Rosalyn said, and thumped him on the back of the head as she went out.

When she closed the door, Edan dropped his pen and leaned back in his chair, rubbing the place she'd thumped him. Maybe he was in a mood again. He'd been stewing in his juices all bloody day.

He stood up and paced around the office. *What in hell are you doing?* Fretting over a woman he scarcely knew? Thinking of holding on to an inn he'd worked so hard to close? All because she'd filled his head with a lot of flowery ideas?

But they were good ideas. So were his.

Edan sat down and tried to work again. But after thirty minutes of that, he gave up. He needed to clear his head. He went outside, Wilbur and Boz trotting along behind him.

And then he watched his dogs trot right past him, all the way down to the first tee box, where Jenny was standing with a golf club in her hand. He heard her exclaim with delight when the dogs appeared, watched her dip down to greet them.

Lorenzo was there with his clubs, too, naturally. So were two women. Tall and slender, the both of them. Pretty. The four of them were laughing, and Lorenzo teed up his ball and took a swing at it, they all cheered for what was obviously a good drive. Next was Jenny's turn. She teed the ball, then swung her club in a haphazard manner. Lorenzo moved in behind her, his body folding over hers, his arms showing her how to swing a golf club.

Edan's blood raced. Had she gone back to that fucking Italian? What was between her and Lorenzo anyway, and why hadn't he bloody well *asked*?

The sudden, piercing shriek of a woman caused Edan to jump a good foot in the air. It sounded as if someone had discovered a body. A sudden commotion and a lot of shouting in Italian followed that when a woman appeared on the walk that went around the inn. She had long, flaming red hair and was wearing a skirt so short that it looked impossible to actually sit. She teetered in heels that made her tower above Ned, who followed along with her bags.

Lorenzo dropped his club. He babbled in Italian, gesturing to Jenny, who was shaking her head, and then raced toward the redhead and grabbed her up, even while the both of them shouted over each other in Italian.

Edan looked back to the women on the tee box.

To his surprise, Jenny was clapping. She was laughing and smiling, clearly happy that this woman had come. And then she was running to where Lorenzo was now kissing the redhead. Incredulous, Edan watched as Lorenzo introduced Jenny, who threw her arms around the woman. And then around Lorenzo. And then around the both of them, pushing them together.

The scene was chaotic and confusing, but Edan was certain of one thing—Jenny was not sleeping with Lorenzo. She wasn't playing both ends against the middle. He turned and walked back to his office, his step a little lighter.

Fifteen

---◆---

Elizabetta was beautiful. A goddess. And a bitch.

She and Lorenzo alternately fought and made up for the rest of the afternoon while Jenny translated for Brooke and Vanessa as best she could. But Lorenzo and Elizabetta's speech was so fast and angry at times that she couldn't keep up. "She's telling him he is as stupid as a cow, and that he thinks with his dick, and he said that she is beautiful and he would do anything for her."

"Like what?" Brooke asked. "I need specifics."

Jenny shook her head. "They're talking too fast. Anyway, I think he's begging like a dog now."

"It's working," Vanessa said, nudging Jenny. The lovebirds were kissing.

"How does that work?" Brooke asked curiously. "How does any of that work?"

Lorenzo seemed happy and loopy in love in spite of the bickering. Elizabetta looked like she wanted to stomp on him some more, but Jenny could see she was warming up to him. There was no question those two belonged with each other.

Jenny wished she had that. Not the volatility, please. But the certainty. She wished for that with all her heart.

It was such a lovely late afternoon that the gathering moved from the golf course to the garden courtyard in front of the inn. Jenny helped Rosalyn round up some champagne and crystal flutes, as Lorenzo had announced that he and Elizabetta were getting married. There wasn't a person among them who believed they'd actually make it to the altar without someone dying, but nevertheless, it was cause to celebrate. Rosalyn and Hugh rounded up Sandra and Ned, and they all came for a toast. Lorenzo's brothers appeared, too, apparently back from the city. No one could seem to find Edan, however.

"You know what?" Vanessa said when they were on their third glass. She was draped across one of the benches, staring up at the turret. "I like it." She glanced at Jenny. "I really like this inn."

"Me too," said Brooke. "I think it could be awesome."

"You do?" Jenny asked, surprised and pleased.

"I do," Vanessa said. "It's quaint. And unique, like you, Jen. I can't wait to see what you do with it."

Jenny smiled broadly. "What do you think, a portable outdoor bar here?" she asked, gesturing to an ivy-covered wall.

"Totally!" Brooke said.

Jenny was explaining her idea for a farm shop

when Vanessa and Brooke's gaze drifted past her. She turned around to see that Edan had come into the courtyard.

"Who is *that*?" Brooke whispered.

"Edan."

Vanessa and Brooke gasped at the exact same moment, at the exact same volume.

Lorenzo, drunk on love, called out to Edan and gestured him over while Elizabetta stood there looking bored. "Come, come, meet the woman who will be my wife."

"*Si matto!*" she said.

"He's crazy," Jenny translated to Vanessa and Brooke.

"Ah but you *will* marry me, *mi amore*," Lorenzo said giddily.

Edan looked like he was walking the plank as he hesitantly walked into the group of Italians and met Elizabetta. He shook her hand, kept the conversation short. Then he looked around, his gaze landing on Jenny.

A shiver of lust ran through her. "Hey," she said.

"Hello," he said back.

Jenny stood up. "These are my friends, Brooke and Vanessa. And this is Edan Mackenzie, the proprietor of the inn."

"*Oh*," Vanessa said, practically falling over herself to extend her hand. "I wasn't expecting *you*," she said.

"I've heard that before," Edan said.

"Your *accent*," Brooke purred.

"Scottish," he said. Edan was perfectly polite, very friendly. He chatted about the weather, and gave a brief history of the inn when Vanessa asked. They asked him about Scotland, and he talked about that, too. Jenny stood there like a dormouse, feeling awkward, unable to add anything to the conversation, her mind racing through all the things she wanted to say to Edan. *Thanks for the hospitality. Oh, before you get on a plane, could you please explain what happened? Because we had such a great time in the sack...*

"I need another drink," Brooke said, wagging her empty flute. "Vanessa, come help me find one."

"I'll fetch it if you like," Edan offered.

"Nope. Need the little girl's room, too," Brooke said, and grabbed Vanessa's arm and made her stand. She smiled at Edan. "*Very* nice to meet you." She dragged Vanessa into the inn.

That left Jenny and Edan standing side by side. The silence between them could not have been more awkward, but this time, Jenny couldn't think of words to fill the silence. "*Sooo,*" she said. "Lorenzo and Elizabetta."

"Aye," he said, glancing over his shoulder at the happy couple, who were now regaling Rosalyn and Hugh with some loud tale.

Edan glanced at Jenny, and he looked...entirely too tentative.

"Okay, enough," Jenny said. "What is the matter with you?"

Edan looked at her as if she'd miraculously sprouted another head. "With *me?*"

"I don't see anyone else standing here."

Edan shook his head. "I, ah..."He shoved his fingers through his hair. Rubbed his chin. Looked around at everyone in the courtyard and said, "I've got to finish some work. And your friends will be back soon. We'll speak later?" He walked into the inn.

Jenny stared at his back, stunned by his awkwardness, his obvious desire to get away from her. "*No,*" she whispered. "You're not getting off the hook that easily." She went after Edan.

She brushed past Vanessa and Brooke returning to the courtyard. "Hey!" Brooke said loudly.

"I'll be back. Wait for me!" Jenny commanded. She kept going, her hands fisting at her sides. She would really like to punch something just now. Preferably Edan's gorgeous face. But she had a few things to say to him first.

She marched in through the door and stood in reception. Not here. Jenny banged on the reception bell, gave it five seconds, and then marched through the door clearly marked "Staff Only" and into his office. Wilbur and Boz were startled by her appearance at his door and leapt to their feet, barking.

Edan leapt to his feet, too. "You nearly scared me out of my wits."

"I rang the bell, but no one came," Jenny said.

"You really need to give a person time to respond," he said.

"Why are you being so weird?" she cried.

Edan sighed. "I've a lot I'm trying to sort through."

"Is that it? Or did you get what you wanted?" Jenny snapped.

Edan's face flushed dark. "*What?*"

"I'm surprised, that's all, and maybe I'm way off here, but I was under the impression you needed a whole lot more than sex. I thought you needed a friend, Edan!"

He snorted. "I donna need a *friend* precisely—"

"Of course not," she interrupted angrily. "Because you're going to run back to your ex. You're going to give up everything you've accomplished here for a woman who doesn't even *want* you. She doesn't love you! Is that the way you want to live your life, chasing after someone who doesn't love you?"

Edan's gaze narrowed. He folded his arms over his chest. "You should no' speak of what you donna know," he said quietly.

"Am I wrong?" she exclaimed loudly. "We had an *amazing* night, Edan—totally, freaking amazing! The stars were shining and little birds were singing, and fairies spun gold around that fucking bed, and you talked to me! You actually *talked.* You opened up and you let yourself breathe, and then, the next morning, *poof*, that man was gone," she said gesturing into the space of that phantom man.

"If you will take a breath and allow me—"

She was not taking a breath until she'd said all she needed to say. "I don't know why you suddenly wanted to pretend nothing had happened between us because it did, and the only reason I can think that you would is because you used me for sex until you can make it back to your *fiancée*."

Edan's face darkened. "Are you quite through?"

Tears welled in her eyes, and if there was one thing she hated, it was tears. "Yes," she said, her voice shaking. "Wait—no. I'll just say this—my dad is coming next week and we're going to make an offer for your inn. You can leave next week. You don't even have to finish closing the inn. You can run, Edan."

His jaw tightened. "Are you through *now*?"

She did a quick rake through her muddled thoughts. "I think so."

"I've been distracted, Jenny, because I've made a decision. The decision is foolish and verra much unlike me, but I've decided I'm not prepared to sell the inn."

Jenny's heart staggered and plummeted in her chest. She couldn't take those words in. For the first time in forever, she had found something to look forward to. She believed she'd found where she belonged, what she was meant to do, and he was going to yank the rug out from her? *Why?* Why would he do that? "What?" she asked weakly, hoping she'd misheard.

"Jenny. I think —"

She hadn't misheard him, and suddenly, she thought if she heard another word, she would be sick. She jerked around, colliding with a cabinet in her haste to get out, tripping over a dog, banging through the door as he called after her.

She fled out to the drive and found Vanessa and Brooke. "I have to get out of here," she said, choking on the words.

"Sure, of course," Vanessa said. "But you need to drive. We're shitfaced."

"Jesus," Jenny muttered. She couldn't even have a decent meltdown without karma interfering.

Sixteen

Edan staggered back to his quarters, his dogs on either side of him like little sentries, as if they expected he was going to fall and they were going to have to drag him to his bed. Frankly, he was surprised he hadn't fallen, because he felt like he'd been hit by a bus.

He'd watched Jenny and her friends speed away from the inn, acutely aware that he couldn't have handled that any worse if he'd tried. What he'd meant to convey was that he was going to stay. *With her.* He wanted to tell her about these new feelings he was having, but damn it if Jenny didn't have an astounding capacity to talk. He hadn't been able to get the words out.

He tossed back two whiskies in quick succession and tried to sort it out.

He did care for Jenny, very much, more than was reasonable. He didn't know why he couldn't say it this morning, or even this afternoon. Why he thought he ought to have a plan for it. Perhaps because he was afraid of his feelings for her? Afraid of pouring everything into a woman only to find out she couldn't abide him? To have his heart shattered all over again? Was it possible that his concern she was involved with Lorenzo a shield he'd given himself so that he wouldn't have to face his own truths?

That sounded ridiculously deep, the sort of thing you heard on lonely heart radio.

Edan didn't know what the truth was, precisely, he only knew that he was drunk and it was dark when he went in search of his flashlight and stumbled up the path to the graveyard.

He'd never been up here at night, and he didn't like it—it was more than a wee bit spooky. But he hadn't known where else to go where he could think, uninterrupted.

He perched on his aunt's headstone. "I've made a mess of things, Clara," he said. "Do you remember how Audra complained I never had much to say? Turns out, I've actually got quite a lot to say, but canna manage to say it."

He watched the dogs sniff about for a moment. "I want to keep the inn, aye? I think I always have. I think I was so afraid of going it alone and, well, I bloody well hate to lose. When Audra left, my pride was hurt, aye? And I didna like the lonely nights, I'll be honest. But then someone amazing came along and everything happened so fast and I couldna get the words out. I have to learn how to get them out, aye? I canna spend my life chatting up a grave."

He suddenly lost his balance and slipped off the headstone and landed on his ass. He sighed and fell onto his back. "I meant no offense, Aunty," he added gruffly. He blinked up at the stars overhead and said, "That's it, then. I'm staying here. Even if Jenny won't stay with me, I'm keeping the bloody inn. There is nothing for me in Scotland now."

He got to his feet and picked up his flashlight. "I miss you more than I can say, Clara. But I must learn to talk to the living." He patted the headstone.

The flashlight flickered then went out.

He banged it against the headstone and it flickered on again.

As Edan made his way down the path to his house, the light went out again. Then fluttered on again. He gave it a shake. Nothing but a strong, steady beam.

He didn't believe in ghosts and spirits. He didn't for a minute think Clara was sending him a signal. But it did make him wonder…what would Clara say if she were here?

Get on with it, Edan, she'd say. He could hear her voice, could see her expression as she said it. *Get on with it, Edan.*

Edan knocked on Rosalyn and Hugh's cottage door at seven o'clock the next morning. Hugh answered in his boxers, a cup of tea in his hand. " Has something happened?"

"Aye," Edan said. "I've got to a wee emergency today. Tell Rosalyn I need her to man the front desk. Sandra will do the cooking."

"Aye, of course," Hugh said. "Are you all right? Can we help?"

"Never better," Edan said, and turned, walking briskly to his car.

He drove straight to the resort and walked up to the reception desk. People were milling about, several of them dressed in tennis togs. A young man was manning the reception desk and smiled when Edan approached. "Good morning, sir, how may I help you?"

"I'm looking for some women."

The young man's brows shot up.

Good Lord. "No' like that," he said with a nervous laugh. "Friends. Their names are Vanessa and Brooke. Two of them, aye? Tall and pretty. One blonde, one brunette."

"Last name?" the man asked.

"Ah...I donna know either surname."

The young man's face turned slightly pink.

"Look, I need to talk to them. If you could just phone up."

"I wouldn't know who to call, sir," he said coolly.

"Fine," Edan said, and tapped his fist on the sleek mahogany reception desk. "Then I'll wait."

He waited until nearly eleven. He had dozed off in a plush easy chair—they could do with chairs like this at the inn—and was jostled awake by someone passing too close. That's when he saw Vanessa walking up the stairs.

He quickly followed her, but couldn't quite catch her before she went into a room.

A few steps behind her, Edan knocked on the door. Several moments passed without a response. He knocked again. This time he heard something hit the floor that sounded like a stack of books, and in the next moment, the door swung open, and Brooke braced herself against the frame, wincing painfully, a palm pressed to her forehead. "*Don't. Knock. Again*," she said darkly.

Her hair looked like a bird's nest. She was wearing a tiny T-shirt and sleep shorts. She squinted at him, and he could see that it took a moment for her to register who he was. "What are *you* doing here?"

"I need to speak to Jenny," he said. "Is she here?" he asked, trying to see past her.

"My God, the lights in this hall are bright," Brooke moaned.

"May I speak to her, please, Brooke?"

"She's not here, Romeo. Vanessa took her back to her room last night. Now go away," she said, and fluttered her hand at him in the signal to go.

God, but he was a bloody idiot. In his haste he hadn't thought to check room 215? He sped back to the inn and strode inside and straight to her room. He knocked loudly, but there was no answer.

"Edan?"

Edan whirled around to see Rosalyn standing behind him with an arm full of linens. "Have you seen Jenny?"

"She's gone on to Black Springs."

Edan blinked. "How? She doesna have a car."

"Lorenzo. He's already back," she said, and nodded in the direction of his room.

Edan walked past Rosalyn and down the hall, to the large room Lorenzo always took. He pounded on the door.

Lorenzo opened it at once. "Good morning, Eddy," he said brightly.

"Where is she?" Edan asked.

"Who?"

"Jenny Turner!" Edan said impatiently. "Where is she?"

"Ah, but she's gone," he said. He suddenly smiled. "My plan, it has worked. See, Elizabetta, my plan has worked!"

Elizabetta said something impatiently in Italian.

"What plan?" Edan asked.

"To make you jealous," Lorenzo said, and poked his chest. "A man, he likes to do the chasing, no?"

Edan grabbed Lorenzo's collar. "Where is she, Lorenzo?"

"Black Springs," he said. "She takes the train."

Edan growled, pushed Lorenzo away, and strode down the hall.

"You are welcome!" Lorenzo shouted after him.

Edan drove like a fiend to Black Springs. He was too late, he had to be too late, but he had to at least try. He pulled into the train station's parking in record time, so fast that he almost collided with a bus. He leapt out and ran into the station, pausing to look at the board. A train to New York was due in ten minutes.

He raced down the train platform to find her. It was Sunday, so there were a lot of weekend travelers headed back to the city, crowding the platform. He hurried through, looking at every face.

Jenny wasn't on the platform. His heart sank. She must have caught an earlier train.

He turned to walk back into the station, racking his brain for what to do next. He'd have to convince Vanessa or Brooke to put him in touch with her, that was what. He felt absolutely ill with regret. And ridiculously stupid. A bloody fool. Hope was slowly bleeding out of him when a conversation filtered into his consciousness.

"My favorite is peanut butter cups. Do you have those here? It's amazing how hard it is to find good junk food at the place I was staying. They need a vending machine if you ask me. People want a little snack from time to time, you know what I mean? I had to beg for a sandwich there once."

"Dollar fifty-four," a male voice said.

"Personally, I prefer the dark chocolate peanut butter cups. They're heart healthy, did you know that? Well, not *healthy*, but, you know, healthier."

Edan slowly turned, his heart beating so rapidly it felt as if it would leap out of his chest. Jenny was standing at a kiosk that sold magazines and candies. He didn't know how he could have missed her—she had on wide-legged trousers that had been tie-dyed, a white T-shirt, and a red sun hat. And, of course, her yoga mat strapped to her back. There were several packages of snack foods on the counter before her and a couple of magazines.

"Jenny," he croaked, but she didn't hear him at first. "*Jenny!*"

She jerked around at her name, her eyes wide. "What are you...? How did you...?"

"I need to speak," he said, sounding like someone who had just crawled out from under a rock. Which fit him, metaphorically.

"*No.*" She turned back to the counter.

"Please, lass. I need to speak. To you."

She sighed. "Fine. Go ahead," she said, and handed the pimply kid a bill. The kid made change, his attention on Edan. He handed it to Jenny then said,

"Say it, dude."

Edan froze. He glanced about. His heart was slamming against his chest. He couldn't possibly say all that was in his heart *here*, in front of everyone. He could hardly say it at all. But when he didn't speak, Jenny shrugged, picked up the bag with her purchases, and started walking toward the platform.

"Jenny, wait."

She stopped. She slowly turned around to face him. Edan couldn't help noticing that several people had slowed to see what was going on, too. Jenny folded her arms, waiting. And she said nothing. At the most inopportune time, she said not a word.

A man strolled by. "*Women,*" he said with vitriol.

Yes, women. Edan couldn't live without this one. He cleared his throat. "When I said I decided not to sell the inn, what I meant to say is that I want to be with you," he blurted.

"*That's* weird," the kid said.

Jenny said nothing.

"I led with the wrong thing," Edan said. "What I was trying to say is that I...I have these feelings," he said, gesturing at his chest. "Strong feelings. I think that you and I would make a great team."

"Oh, it's a *job* interview," the kid said.

Jenny reached into her bag and took out a candy bar and began to unwrap it.

Edan closed his eyes a moment. "Jenny... I have never met a woman like you, aye? You've opened my eyes to possibilities in my life I never saw before. I donna want you to go."

She looked up from her candy bar, and still she said nothing. She was suddenly mute? Had she finally run out of words to utter? After the hundreds upon thousands of words she'd used this week, *now* was the time the well would run dry? Was she just going to stand there and let him twist at the end of his rope? "I…I donna know what to say—"

Jenny rolled her eyes and turned to walk away.

"Except that I want you to stay!" he called after her. "You are a light that appeared in my dismal existence! You opened the windows and let the air in! Do you want the full truth, then? Brace yourself, lass, for you may no' care for it. But the full truth is that I am falling in love with you!"

Someone behind him cooed with delight.

Jenny stopped walking. She turned halfway back, her lips parted with surprise.

"I donna know how it will work, you and I—but I know that I canna let you get on that train without asking you to stay and at least see what happens between us."

The announcement that a train was approaching the station flooded Edan with panic. Had he said all that he needed to say? Was it enough? Had he said the right things? He moved close enough to her now that he could catch her hand. He squeezed her fingers, laced his with hers. "I'm asking you, from the bottom of my heart, to stay and see if this magic between us is real."

Her eyes lit, but still she did not speak.

Edan groaned. "Why do you no' *speak*?"

"Because what you're saying is so *beautiful*, I don't want to ruin it," she said, and then smiled with the force of a thousand suns. "I'll stay, Edan, are you kidding me? You need me so bad." She threw her arms around his neck, then planted her luscious lips on his. "And I need you, too," she said into his ear.

Edan kissed her with all that he was feeling in the middle of that train station. He didn't care that people were gawking. He didn't care when one old man admonished them to take their inappropriate behavior to a private room. He only cared that Jenny was in his arms, and she was kissing him. And he couldn't wait to get her home, he couldn't wait to make love to her again, he couldn't wait to see how far they could go together.

He sincerely hoped he didn't have to express that in words. But there seemed to be no danger, for Jenny was suddenly talking about whale pods, something about how they stuck together through storms and calm seas.

Get on with it, Edan.

Epilogue

*S*ix months later

    Everyone had come for the groundbreaking of the new spa and farm shop at the Cassian Inn, made possible by a generous loan from Jenny's father. This was just the beginning—they had grand plans, Jenny and Edan, beginning with a wedding that would take place in the summer.

    "So soon?" Bethany asked. She had come along with Vanessa and Brooke for the party.

    "Why not?" Jenny asked. "We're going to do it here, in the new salon." After much discussion, and a desire not to live where Edan had once lived with Audra, Edan and Jenny had taken the cottage up on the hill and had turned the private quarters into a premiere suite and a new, larger salon. They'd hung crystal chandeliers, had painted the paneling a soft gray, and had replaced the carpets and furnishings.

The best part of their work so far was the addition of a small bar in the new salon. It was now Jenny's favorite room in the old mansion.

"Did I tell you about the woman who is going to marry us?" she said to her friends. "She's a mystic. She read our cards and she said—"

"You've told me, like, one hundred times," Bethany said, and smiled at the others. Jenny supposed that look was because she hadn't stopped talking since they'd arrived. Could they blame her? She was deliriously happy.

She glanced at her watch—the ceremony would begin shortly. "I've got to get out there and greet people. You know how Edan is," she said with a warm smile. "He'll say hello and think he's done. I'll probably have to carry the whole event."

"Thank God you're so good at this sort of thing," Vanessa said with a laugh.

The four women walked out of the inn and around to the first tee, which, to the consternation of the four seniors who met every Saturday to play, was being used today for the groundbreaking ceremony. The crowd was thick—people around Lake Haven and from East Beach had come to have a look at the plans and witness the ribbon cutting, arriving on the shuttle Jenny had negotiated with the village of East Beach. A shuttle that ran all around the lake had proven so popular that the village was going to expand the service from two to three trips a day during the high season.

After the short ceremony, there would be a reception to showcase the things that would be available in the new farm shop. Who knew that Sandra had been desperate to open one? Edan hadn't realized it, but Jenny had. Sandra was in her element and had baked so many cakes that Jenny had been haunted by the scent of chocolate all week.

A pregnant Rosalyn and Hugh were in attendance. They'd decided to give the inn another year before deciding if they'd move to the city. Jenny and Rosalyn had become very good friends, and Jenny was certain they would stay. Ned and Sandra had come, the two old friends who still shared the farmhouse. It seemed Ned was not ready to retire just yet, and Sandra had not wanted to leave the spot where Clara was buried. Edan had arranged for Mr. Finlay to be brought down from the senior home. "I donna know what he recognizes, but he was as much a part of the inn as anyone," he'd told Jenny. The old man didn't know where he was, but he was enchanted with Wilbur and Boz, they, in turn, were enchanted with his attention to them.

Jenny's father had come with Cathy and her teenage son, who skulked around Vanessa and Brooke most of the time. Even Lorenzo had come back for the ribbon cutting. Not with his one and only true love, Elizabetta, but with his new one and only true love, the doe-eyed, slinky Tatyana. "She is the love of my life, this girl," he'd whispered to Jenny.

Jenny walked up to Edan, who was reviewing some note cards. He looked magnificent in his formal kilt. "How do I look?" he asked as he took her hand and kissed her cheek.

"Sexy," she said. "So *sexy.* You should wear that to bed."

He frowned. "I hoped to appear a bit mayoral."

"That's totally what I meant," she said with a laugh. "Are you ready, Mr. Mackenzie? People are dying for champagne and nutballs."

"*Och,* donna talk dirty to me now, love," he said. With a squeeze of her hand, they walked to the little platform Ned had put up and signaled that the ceremony was to begin.

"I'll start," Edan whispered to her.

"Okay, you do that," Jenny said. She would fill in when necessary as she always did.

"Thank you all for coming today," Edan said when he'd gained everyone's attention. "This," he said, gesturing to the place where the shop and spa would be built, "was an idea only a few months ago." He paused.

Jenny shifted forward, prepared to fill in, but Edan put his hand on her arm.

"Like all good ideas, it needed time to germinate, aye? For roots to sink and grow."

Again, he hesitated, and again, Jenny tried to step forward. But Edan's hand was still on her arm, and he squeezed it.

"But the time has come for new growth and tourism around Lake Haven. We at the Cassian Inn intend to be a part of that growth and continued history. What we mean to do here will only enhance what we all do, together, as a community. We've a plan for it..."

Edan continued to talk about growth and change. Jenny watched him, amazed at his many words. Amazed that this was the same man who had scarcely spoken a word the night she had arrived. She was so proud to be by his side. So bloody proud, as he would say. So thoroughly in love.

When he ended an amazing eight minutes of speaking, she and Edan cut the ribbon to enthusiastic applause.

"Come on, then, the lot of you, to the courtyard for champagne!" Rosalyn called to the assembly.

Edan and Jenny stood back, watching their neighbors and friends and staff make their way to the courtyard. "That was fabulous," Jenny said. "*You* were fabulous, Edan."

He smiled at her with such adoration that her skin began to tingle. "I could never have done this without you, lass. To think of all the years I muddled through, trying to please those who could no' be pleased."

"I know," she said. "That's just what I was—"

"To think I might have gone on that way for the rest of my bloody life," he interrupted, and shook his head. "God, but I love you, Jen."

"And I love—"

"We will fill this inn with babies and dogs and friends and family, aye? You belong here, with me, and we belong together, always. Do you know what? I believe in fate. You've made me believe in it. Come, we best have a bit of champagne before they drink us dry. I know how your friends are." He gathered her in his arms and kissed her fully, then hand-in-hand, they went down to the courtyard.

Jenny was so happy that she didn't care she hadn't managed to get a single word in today.

Life was so lovely, and the best part was that she finally knew where to start.

THE END

Excerpt from
SUDDENLY ENGAGED

A Lake Haven Novel Book 3
by Julia London

———◆———

Leave it to a female to think the rules did not apply to her.

The little heathen from next door was crawling under the split-rail fence that separated the cottages again. Dax, who already had been feeling pretty damn grumpy going on a year now, wondered why she didn't just go over the fence. She was big enough. It was almost as if she wanted the mud on her dress and her knees, to drag the ends of her dark red ponytails through the muck.

She crawled under, stood up, and knocked the caked mud off her knees. She stomped her pink, sparkly cowboy boots—never had he seen a more impractical shoe—to make them light up, as she liked to do, hopping around her porch several times a day.

Then she started for cottage Number Two, arms swinging, stride long.

Dax watched her from inside his kitchen, annoyed. It had started a week ago, when she'd climbed on the bottom railing of the fence, leaned over it, and shouted, "I like your dog!"

He'd ignored her.

Two days ago he'd asked her, fairly politely, not to give any more cheese to his dog, Otto. That little stunt of hers had resulted in a very long and malodorous night between man and beast.

Yesterday he'd commanded her to stay on her side of the fence.

But here the little monster came, apparently neither impressed with him nor intimidated by his warnings.

Well, Dax had had enough with that family, or whatever the situation was next door. *And* the enormous pickup truck that showed up at seven a.m. and idled in the drive just outside his bedroom window. Those people were exactly what was wrong with America—people doing whatever they wanted without regard for anyone else, letting their kids run wild, coming and going at all hours of the day.

He walked to the back screen door and opened it. He'd installed a dog door, but Otto refused to use it. No, Otto was a precious buttercup of a dog that liked to have his doors opened for him, and he assumed that anytime Dax neared the door, it was to open it for him. He assumed so now, stepping in front of Dax— pausing to stretch after his snoring nap—before sauntering out and down the back porch steps to sniff something at the bottom.

Dax walked out onto the porch and stood with his hands on his hips as the girl brazenly advanced.

"Hi!" she said.

She was about to learn that she couldn't make a little girl's social call whenever she wanted. There were rules in this world, and Dax had no compunction about teaching them to her. Clearly someone needed to. He responded to her greeting with a glower.

"Hi!" she said again, shouting this time, as if he hadn't heard her from the tremendous distance of about six feet.

"What'd I tell you yesterday?" he asked.

"To stay on the other side of the fence."

"Then why are you over here?"

"I forgot." She rocked back on her heels and balanced on them, toes up. "Do you live there?"

"No, I just stand on the porch and guard the fence. *Yes*, I live here. And I work here. And I don't want visitors. Now go home."

"My name is Ruby Kokinos. What's yours?"

What was wrong with this kid? "Where is your mother?"

"At work."

"Then is your dad home?"

"My daddy is in Africa. He teaches cats to do tricks," she said, pausing to twirl around on one heel. "*Big* cats, not little cats. They have really big cats in Africa."

"Whatever," he said impatiently. "Who is home with you right now?"

"Mrs. Miller. She's watching TV. She said I could go outside."

Great. A babysitter. "Go home," he said, pointing to Number Three as Otto wandered over to examine

Ruby Coconuts, or whatever her name was. "Go home and tell Mrs. Miller that you're not allowed to come over or under that fence. Do you understand me?"

"What's your dog's name?" she asked, petting that lazy, useless mutt.

"Did you hear me?" Dax asked.

"Yes." She giggled as Otto began to lick her hand, and went down on her knees to hug him. "I *always always* wanted a dog, but Mommy says I can't have one now. Maybe when I'm big." She stroked Otto's nose, and the dog sat, settling in for some attention.

"Don't pet the dog," Dax said. "I just told you to go home. What else did I tell you to do?"

"To, um, to tell Mrs. Miller to stay over there," she said, as she continued to pet the dog. "What's her name?"

"It's a he, and his name is Otto. And I told you to tell Mrs. Miller that *you* are supposed to stay over there. Now go on."

She stopped petting the dog, and Otto, not ready for the gravy train of attention to end, began to lick her face. Ruby giggled with delight. Otto licked harder, like she'd been handling red meat. Frankly, it wouldn't surprise Dax if she had—the kid seemed like the type to be into everything. She was laughing uncontrollably now and fell onto her back. Otto straddled her, his tail wagging as hard as her feet were kicking, trying to lick her while she tried to hold him off.

Nope, this was not going to happen. Those two useless beings were not making friends. Dax marched down off the porch and grabbed Otto's collar, shoving him out of the way. *"Go,"* he said to the dog, pointing to his cottage. Otto obediently lumbered away.

Dax turned his attention to the girl with the fantastically dark red hair in two uneven pigtails and, now that he was close to her, he could see her clear blue eyes through the round lenses of her blue plastic eyeglasses, which were strapped to her face with a headband. She looked like a very young little old lady. "Listen to me, kid. I don't want you over here. I work here. Serious work. I can't be entertaining little girls."

She hopped to her feet. "What's your name?"

Dax sighed. "If I tell you my name, will you go home?"

She nodded, her, long pigtails bouncing around her.

"Dax."

She stared at him.

"That's my name," he said with a shrug.

Ruby giggled and began to sway side to side. "That's not a real name!"

"It's as real as Ruby Coconuts."

"Not *Coconuts!*" She squealed with delight. "It's Ruby *Kokinos.*"

"Yeah, okay, but I'm pretty sure you said *Coconuts.* Now go home."

"How old are you?"

"I'm a lot older than you," he said and put his hands on her shoulders, turning her around.

"I'm going to be seven on my birthday. I want a Barbie for my birthday. I already have four. I want the one that has the car. The *pink* car with flowers on it. There's a *blue* car, but I don't want that one, I want the *pink* one, because it has flowers on it. Oh, and guess what, I don't want a Jasmine anymore. That's my favorite princess, but I don't want her anymore, I want a Barbie like Taleesha has."

"Great. Good luck with that," he said as he moved her toward the fence.

"My shoes light up," she informed him, stomping her feet as they moved. "My mom says they're fancy. They're my favorites. I have some sneakers, too, but they don't light up."

They had reached the fence, thank God, before the girl could give him a rundown of her entire shoe collection. Ruby dipped down, apparently thinking she'd go under again, but Dax caught her under her arms and swung her over the fence, depositing her on the other side.

Ruby laughed with delight. "Do that again!"

"No. This is where our acquaintance comes to an end, kid. I don't have time to babysit you, get it?"

"Yes," she said.

She didn't get it. She wasn't even listening. She had already climbed onto the bottom rail, as if she meant to come back over.

"I mean it," he said, pointing at her. "If I find you on my side of the fence, I'm going to call the police." He figured that ought to put the fear of God into her.

"The policemans are our friends," she said sunnily. "A policeman and a police woman came to my kindergarten. But they never shot any peoples."

Dax had a brief but potent urge to correct her understanding of how plurals worked, but he didn't. He turned around and marched back to his cottage.

He didn't even want to look out the kitchen window when he went inside, because if she'd come back over the fence, he would lose it.

He'd known that family was going to be trouble the moment they'd arrived a few days ago. They'd cost him a table leg he'd been working on, because they'd slammed a door so loudly and unexpectedly that Dax had started, and the permanent marker he was using to outline a very intricate pattern on said table leg had gone dashing off in a thick, black, indelible line down the leg. He'd had to sand the leg down and start again.

Naturally, he'd gone to investigate the source of the banging, and he'd seen a woman with a backpack strapped to her leaning into the open hatch area of a banged-up Subaru. She'd pulled out a box, hoisted it into her arms with the help of her knee, then lugged it up the path and porch steps to Number Three. She'd been wearing short shorts, a T-shirt, and a ball cap. Dax hadn't seen her face, but he'd seen her legs, which were nice and long and shapely, and a mess of dark hair about the same color as wrought iron, tangled up in the back of the cap. She'd managed to open the door, and then had gone in, letting the door bang behind her.

Neighbors. Dax was not a fan.

The door of Number Three had continued to bang away most of the afternoon, and Dax had been unable to work. He'd stood at the kitchen sink, eating from a can of peanuts, watching the woman jog down the front porch steps, then lug something else inside. He'd noticed other things about her. Like how her ass was bouncy and her figure had curves in all the right places, and how her T-shirt hugged her. He'd noticed that she looked really pretty from a distance, with wide eyes and dark brows and full lips.

Of course he'd also noticed the little monster, who'd spent most of the afternoon doing a *clomp clomp clomp* around the wooden porch in those damn pink cowboy boots.

Kids. If anything could make Dax grumpier, it was a cute kid.

He'd turned away from the window in a bit of a snit. Of course he was used to people renting any one of the six East Beach Lake Cottages around him for a week or two, and usually they had kids. He much preferred the olds who took up weekly residence from time to time, couples with puffs of white hair, sensible shoes, and early bedtimes. Families on vacation were loud, their arguments drifting in through the windows Dax liked to keep open.

The cottages were at the wrong end of Lake Haven, which made them affordable. But they were at the right end of beauty—each of them faced the lake, and a private, sandy beach was only a hundred feet or so from their front porches. He'd been lucky to find this place, with its unused shed out back, which he'd negotiated to use. He had to remind himself that his setup was perfect when new people showed up and banged their doors open and shut all damn day.

Dax had realized that afternoon, as the banging had undone him, that the woman and kid were moving *in*—no one hauled that much crap into a cottage for a vacation. He'd peered out the kitchen window, trying to assess exactly how much stuff was going into that cottage. But by the time he did, the Subaru was closed up, and he didn't see any signs of the woman and the kid.

He'd wandered outside for a surreptitious inspection of what the hell was happening next door when the door suddenly banged open and the mom came hurrying outside. She'd paused on the bottom step of the porch when she saw him. Her dark hair had spilled around her shoulders and her legs had taunted him, all smooth and shapely and long in those short shorts. *Don't look*, those legs shouted at him. *Don't look, you pervert, don't look!* Dax hadn't looked. He'd studied the keys in her hand.

"Hi," she'd said uncertainly.

"Hi."

She kept smiling. Dax kept standing there like an imbecile. She leaned a little and looked around him, to Number Two. "Are you my neighbor?"

"What? Oh, ah...yeah. I'm Dax."

"Hi, Dax. I'm Kyra," she'd said. That smile of hers, all sparkly and bright, had made him feel funny inside. Like he'd eaten one of those powdered candies that crackled when it hit your mouth.

"I wondered about my neighbors. It's pretty quiet around here. I saw a car in front of one of the cottages down there," she said, pointing.

"Five," he said.

"What?"

He'd suddenly felt weirdly conspicuous, seeing as how he was standing around with nothing to do. "That's Five," he said, to clarify.

"Ah."

"You're in Three. I'm in Two."

He'd been instantly alarmed by what he was doing, explaining the numbering system on a series of six cottages. She'd looked as if she'd expected him to say more. When he hadn't said anything, but sort of nodded like a mute, she'd said, "Okay, well...nice to meet you," and had hurried on to her car much like a woman would hurry down a dark street with some stranger walking briskly behind her. She opened the door, leaned in...nice view...then emerged holding a book. She locked the door, then ran past him with a weird wave before disappearing inside.

Dax had told himself to get a grip. There was nothing to panic over.

He hadn't panicked until much later that afternoon, when he'd happened to glance outside and had seen a respectable pile of empty moving boxes on the front porch and the little monster trying to build a house out of them.

That was definitely a long-term stay. And he didn't like that, not one bit.

He'd managed to keep busy and avoid his new neighbors for a few days, but then, yesterday, the truck had shown up, treating him to the sound of a large HEMI engine idling near his bedroom window.

He'd let it pass, figuring that it was someone visiting.

But it happened again. Just now.

Dax was in the middle of a good dream when that damn truck pulled in. He groggily opened his eyes, noticed the time. It was a good hour before he liked to get up. Was this going to be a regular thing, then? He groaned and looked to his right; Otto was sitting next to the bed, staring at Dax, his tail thumping. "Use the damn dog door, Otto," he tried, but that only excited the dog. He jumped up and put his big mutt paws on Dax.

With a grunt, Dax pushed the dog aside, then staggered into the kitchen. He heaped some dog food into a metal bowl and put it on the ground. In the time it took him to fire up the coffeepot, Otto had eaten his food and was standing at the back door, patiently waiting.

Dax opened the door. He glanced over to Three.

The Subaru was gone, and he couldn't help wonder who was driving that massive red truck. A husband? A dad? Jesus, he hoped the guy wasn't the chatty type. *Hey neighbor, whatcha working on over there?*

Yeah, Dax was in no mood for more neighbors or barbecue invitations or neighborly favors. But it was becoming clear to him that little Miss Ruby Coconuts was going to make his policy of isolationism really difficult.

Dax got dressed and went out to the shed to work. A few hours later he walked into the kitchen to grab some rags he'd washed in the sink and happened to look out his kitchen window.

The redheaded devil was hanging upside down off the porch railing of her house, her arms reaching for the ground. She was about three inches short, however, and for a minute Dax was certain she would crash headlong into that flowerbed and hurt herself. But she didn't. She managed to haul herself up and hopped off the railing. And then she looked across the neat little lawn to Dax's cottage.

"Don't even *think* about it," he muttered.

Ruby hesitated. She slid her foot off the porch and onto the next step down. Then the other foot. She leapt to the ground from there, looking down, admiring the lights in her shoes. Then she looked up at his cottage again.

"Don't do it, you little monster. *Don't you dare do it.*"

Ruby was off like a shot, headed for the fence.

END OF EXCERPT

About The Author

Julia London is the *New York Times, USA Today,* and *Publisher's Weekly* best-selling author of more than forty romantic fiction novels. She is the author of the critically acclaimed *Highland Grooms* historical series, including *Wild Wicked Scot, Sinful Scottish Laird, Hard-Hearted Highlander Devil In Tartan, Tempting The Laird and Seduced By A Scot.* She is also the author of several contemporary romances, including the *Homecoming Ranch Series and the Suddenly series, including Suddenly Dating, Suddenly in Love, and Suddenly Engaged.*

Julia is the recipient of the RT Bookclub Award for Best Historical Romance and a six time finalist for the prestigious RITA award for excellence in romantic fiction.

She lives in Austin, Texas.

Visit Julia's Websiste
http://julialondon.com

Fnd Julia on Facebook
https://www.facebook.com/JuliaLondonAuth

Follow Julia on Twitter
https://twitter.com/juliaflondon